fragile boys, fragile men

Canadä

*The Publishers acknowledge the financial assistance of the
Government of Canada through the Book Publishing Industry
Development Program (BPIDP) for our publishing activities.*

Library and Archives Canada Cataloguing in Publication

Griffin, Harold, 1936-
    Fragile boys, fragile men / Harold Griffin.

ISBN 978-0-88887-359-0

    1. Irish Canadians—Québec (Province)—Québec—Fiction.
I. Title.

PS8613.R537F73 2008   C813'.6   C2008-903063-X

Cover photo: Jean-Paul Lemieux
              "Young Man Reading", 1927?
              National Gallery of Canada, Ottawa
              Photo © NGC

Printed and bound in Canada on acid free paper.

fragile boys, fragile men

Harold Griffin

Borealis Press
Ottawa, Canada
2008

To my wife Helen, my daughter Kathleen,
and my sons Aidan, Dylan and Benjamin

Contents

I would like to thank Frank M. Tierney for his encouragement and good humour, as well as Janet Shorten for her invaluable advice and "adjustments" to my manuscript.

I am indebted to the following people for their advice regarding this project: Daniel Griffin (my older brother), June Wilkins, Rick Cochrane, and Claire Duchesneau. My brother, Joseph Griffin, has given me guidance and counsel. My gratitude to Dylan Griffin and Amy Fecteau for their support and hospitality.

But most of all, I thank my wife, Helen, who has to put up with me every day.

Introduction

Most of the stories in this collection deal with the circumstances of certain Canadian Irish families, descendants of immigrants who came to Canada in the early 1800s. The fictionalized accounts begin during the Second World War, and move forward.

Back in 1820, Seigneur Michel Louis Juchereau Duchesnay opened up his seigneury to Irish tenant-farmers in an area some twenty miles north of Quebec City. This community was called the St. Patrick Settlement. To assist the settlers, Seigneur Duchesnay liberally "advanced them provision and seed, opened roads, and procured work for some and employed others himself." No capital was needed to acquire the land, and no rent was expected until after three years.

Over the ensuing decades, Irish settlers did achieve full ownership of their lands through much toil and sacrifice. The area then came to be known as Shannon, named after the river in Ireland, or Valcartier (Vallée de la Jacques-Cartier), which referred to the broader area surrounding the Irish community. The settlers were very committed to their Catholic faith and built up the parish of St. Catherine, as well as a smaller congregation, St. Gabriel's, in Valcartier Village, the area they shared with the descendants of United Empire Loyalists and Scottish immigrants.

Much of the land originally granted to the Irish settlers was expropriated during the First World War for the establishment of the Valcartier Military Camp. Then again in 1965 the federal government took more land.

1

Some of the Irish felt that their land had been "pillaged." But living near the camp has at least given employment to people in the Shannon area. The camp also provides school in English and French, so that Irish-Anglo culture continues to survive in the area.

Generally speaking, most of the Irish immigrants had sizable families. Since the farms could not sustain the children when they grew into adulthood, the young men and women went to the cities of Quebec, to other parts of Canada, and to the United States to acquire employment.

In the province of Quebec the Irish had been welcomed by francophones. The francophones had adopted Irish orphans who had lost their parents during the Irish Famine of the 1840s.

"They were our best friends," said the late Eddie Conway, a former mayor of Shannon. "They took care of us when there was no one else. The British had nothing but disdain for us." So there was some inter-marriage between the Irish and the francophones, especially into the turn of the twentieth century.

While he was alive, Eddie Conway accumulated a collection forming an early photographic history of the Irish in the district.

Irish surnames are still evident in Quebec City, and the ancestors of the early Shannon immigrants—people in these narratives—are, perhaps distantly, related to one another.

Not all of the occurrences in these stories eventuate into satisfactory outcomes, but the distinctive features of their "heroes" are present for all to see.

The last three stories in this collection are more contemporary in nature, and not connected to the first seven stories.

Benjamin Kerwin

BENJAMIN KERWIN was proud of his father during those Second World War years when his dad was a gate keeper at the munitions plant. The boy saw this as an important position, although in reality his father was part of a rather primitive security system. One of his father's obligations was to request that shift workers leaving the plant open their lunch pails as they exited the gate, allowing him to take a quick peek inside the containers to make sure workers weren't stealing bullets, or anything else.

The munitions plant, Canadian Arsenals Inc., was right in the centre of the old city, a ten-minute walk from the family's second-story flat. Benjamin Kerwin's mom would sometimes send him to deliver something to his father at the gate of the factory, perhaps a brown bag containing a sandwich his dad had forgotten.

It was a chore that the boy did not complain about. His father's eyes lit up when Benjamin would knock on the door of the small booth just inside the high steel fence. That was one of the things that the boy loved about his father. Benjamin was made to feel like a long-lost relative every time he visited the plant, where he would be introduced to other workers who might saunter by, including some uniformed guards.

"This is my fourth son, Benjamin," the father would boast.

"Tiens! Bonjour Benjamin!" the guard would say with some ebullience, and give Benjamin a firm handshake.

Benjamin's father, Michael Kerwin, held his job through the long war years, bringing home a modest but steady salary. This was a welcome change from the years before the war, when the Depression, with its periods of high unemployment, had made life near-desperate for the growing family. Michael, who had been raised on a farm some twenty-five miles north of Quebec City, had left his own homestead as a young man to secure work, wood-cutting and logging throughout Quebec, and working the harvests of western Canada. Most of the jobs he would get were temporary. He had no marketable trade, and only a grade six education. But he was a fit and wiry man who could put in a hard day's work.

While working in northern Quebec—the French-speaking Lac St. Jean area—Michael met his wife-to-be. In January of 1928 he was employed at a sawmill in Riverbend, a town near St. Joseph d'Alma where Rosalie Bouchard was working as a grocery clerk. They met in a Catholic Church basement, at a parish social, one Saturday evening.

To describe Michael's understanding of French as rudimentary would have been a leap of faith. Her knowledge of English was at a similar level. Yet they managed to convey to each other that, as unattached people, they might see each other again.

As it turned out, Michael's use of French improved very little, a victim of some neglect on his part. Rosalie, on the other hand, embraced the English language and in the ensuing years she would learn to speak, read, and write it without too much difficulty.

Michael and Rosalie married and had their first child—a boy. Then, unfortunately, Michael's job at the sawmill was terminated. They decided to move to Quebec City, where they thought employment opportunities would be better. Here Michael was closer to the Irish community, Shannon, where he had been raised.

Despite the dire economic conditions of the ongoing Depression, and the resultant hard times, Michael and Rosalie accepted the children born to them with resolve and dedication. Michael was adamant in his pursuit of work, doing odd jobs, and always making himself available when public works projects were started by the municipal authorities during summer and winter.

In the winter of early 1945, Benjamin Kerwin was the fourth of six children residing in a rented second-storey walk-up, a flat with two bedrooms.

St. Patrick's High School, so named, which Benjamin attended as a grade five student, was a school for boys only, and was run by the Christian Brothers of St. John the Baptist de la Salle. The Brothers, highly revered in the parish of St. Patrick's, taught all grades in elementary and high school, along with a group of lay teachers. The school was a fifteen-minute walk from the Kerwin household. And then, of course, Benjamin and his older siblings always walked home for a hot lunch at noon—food which their mother Rosalie meticulously prepared.

During the winter months this routine was a hard grind for the children, including one younger sister who was now old enough to attend the girls' school. But the children of Michael Kerwin thrived on this regimen, and were active in the sports programs at school as well.

Benjamin and two of his brothers, Tom and Mike (Junior), played hockey in the house league at school.

They were talented players and they played on the top school teams which competed against other schools.

Benjamin's older brother Mike had also joined the ranks of the work force as of the previous autumn of 1944. He had signed up with the Montreal *Gazette* to deliver the morning paper to over thirty-five households, all situated within the old walled section of Quebec City. This route was followed daily, with the exception of Sunday. The *Gazette* did not publish on Sunday. As his brother's helper, Benjamin was paid two dollars weekly from the cash that his brother collected every Saturday.

Rising at six a.m. on frigid winter mornings was the most difficult part of the job for the two boys. After an overnight snowfall, they were likely to be the first to break the smooth surfaces of whiteness, even before the snowploughs appeared and while the crisp dawn brightened into day. They would trudge up to the Clarendon Hotel to where their newspapers had been dropped off, bound together in a bundle just inside the main entrance of the hotel.

From then on it was a race for them to get the newspapers delivered to the doorways, get home to eat some breakfast, and then head off to school.

English-speaking readers were a small minority in Quebec City, so Mike's subscribers to the Montreal newspaper were widespread among the ancient historic streets. The boys noticed that most of these people lived in well-kept houses with slanting roofs, large windows, and shiny brass-coloured door knobs. They were mostly of old English stock, with names like Price and Fraser and Goodfellow. Some of the subscribers paid directly to the *Gazette* in Montreal, so Mike and Benjamin seldom got to see them in person; they collected from the other subscribers on Saturdays.

Christmas of 1944 had been a boon for the boys. Most of the customer-subscribers had tipped them generously. One lady had given them a five-dollar bill, which seemed ultra-magnanimous. After collecting just before Christmas, Mike had counted his bounty and had given Benjamin ten dollars. This was enough to enable Benjamin to buy himself a new pair of skates, to replace the battered pair that had been handed down to him from his older brother Tom. With his new acquisition Benjamin had skated every day at St. Patrick's rink over the Christmas holiday period of two weeks.

The rink was maintained and flooded nightly by a man employed for this purpose by the parish that owned the property next to St. Patrick's school. During the Christmas holidays there were periods of recreational skating in the afternoons and evenings for families and young people. Benjamin and his buddies from school availed themselves of this activity daily, doing a lot of socializing, along with whizzing around the rink and honing their skills as skaters.

Benjamin also played hockey about every two days in the school house league which ran a schedule all through the winter months. He was the second highest scorer in the house league—Pee-Wee division. He loved hockey and anything connected with it.

Skating was probably the greatest skill of the eleven-year-old player. For Benjamin, it was another dimension of life to be on his blades, where he could perform better than most of his peers. His skates were a second pair of feet for him, enabling him to manoeuvre freely. He could skate at full speed, then stop quickly, using one or both feet. He could skate backwards with facility and good control, and then whirl away, reaching for that quickness which was so necessary to excel. To do all of these things while controlling the puck with his hockey stick—that was what he worked hard to achieve. He was mesmerized by the game, and, with his brothers, seized every opportunity to play street hockey during all kinds of weather most of the year.

The Kerwin family lived in rather cramped conditions in their second-storey five-room flat. The neighbours below them were a childless francophone married couple who frequently complained, usually to Rosalie, about the noise generated by the young family of "anglais." As a result, a strained relationship existed between the two tenant households. Rosalie, speaking in her native French, would offer apologies for the discordant activities of her children, but she wasn't about to get down on her knees to do it. Rosalie did not consider the behaviour of her boys to be abnormally disruptive.

Since Michael Kerwin worked in eight-hour shifts, he frequently was absent from the flat overnight. He preferred the eight-to-four daytime shift, which enabled him to be with his family at suppertime and in the evening. When he worked the night shifts, the children knew that their father required a quiet daytime. Rosalie, of course, was constantly warning them.

"Quiet now! Let your father sleep," she would say, her voice hushed, when the talk became rowdy or rancorous.

If arguments or fights broke out at noontime while Michael was trying to sleep, he would open the bedroom door and stand in his longjohns staring at the boys.

For sleeping accommodations, the two young girls, Cheryl and Kathleen, shared one of the bedrooms with their parents, while three of the boys occupied the other bedroom. Benjamin slept in the hallway, on a sofa bed. He liked it there, and read his "chapter" books using the available light and occasionally watching his mother through an open doorway as she sat, usually knitting and listening to her favourite French radio programs, many featuring classical music softly playing and lulling him to sleep.

Benjamin was also an altar boy at St. Patrick's Parish Church, and frequently served at one of the Sunday Masses. He also was required to serve, as part of a team of altar boys, for a week-long period at early daily Mass about once every six weeks. If he was occupied with this, he could not help his brother with the newspaper route. He would therefore be deprived of the money he normally earned, but it was a sacrifice that he was willing to make.

The teaching Brothers at school had been impressed at how fast Benjamin had memorized the Latin responses required of altar boys. Benjamin had never missed a serving assignment, and with his partner Alan Kane was proud to don the soutane and surplice for any altar service. Besides, they were a couple of clowns and enjoyed each other's company.

Benjamin and Alan were grade five classmates at St. Patrick's and played hockey together on the same house league team. They especially enjoyed talking about the idiosyncrasies of their teacher, Mr. Shaw, one of the lay teachers at the school, who would often tell his students stories of his own experiences. Mr. Shaw said he'd been a boxer as a younger man and he loved to describe some of the ring battles he'd had.

"How did you win the fight, Mr. Shaw?" one of the boys would ask.

"Just kept moving, kept moving. Then came in quick with a left jab and followed it up, fast, with a right hook. He was down before he knew what happened. Paying attention all the time, that's the secret, boys," Mr. Shaw told his enthralled audience.

This mesmerizing grip on impressionable young boys was achieved because Mr. William Shaw was willing to digress from normal subject matter. He saw education, in part, as a discussion of experience, and could not resist the temptation to talk about his own difficulties as a boy and a young man. His students had great respect for him and many would later say that they discovered a love of learning while under his tutelage.

St. Patrick's High School was a school for working-class Irish families. The Irish had long been evident in Quebec City, having served with British forces in 1759 when the British had defeated the French to take control of the old city in what was later to become part of the province of Quebec in Canada. In the early 1800s, Irish immigrants began arriving in greater numbers. Some of them settled in the city, but the great-great-grandfather of Benjamin Kerwin, when he landed at the dock in 1824 with his young family, was given the right to develop a plot of land, as a tenant farmer, amounting to about 220 acres in an area north of the old city. This acreage, much of which was arboreal, had to be cleared so that homesteads could be built and gardens and crops sown. The area where the land was located was known as the St. Patrick Settlement because of the numerous Irish immigrants who had begun to settle there.

Within the old city itself, the Irish had begun to make their mark by the middle and late 1800s. They were a gritty, hard-working, resilient people.

By the late 1800s a large proportion of police officers in the Quebec City Police Department were of Irish descent.

The francophone citizens of Quebec had accepted the Irish into their midst. After all, it was the Seigneur Duchesnay who had opened up his seigneury to Irish settlers in 1820. At the height of the Irish Potato Famine in the 1840s, many francophone families had adopted Irish orphans who had lost their parents to diseases, contracted while shipping out of Ireland in a mass exodus. Because both French-Canadians and Irish were Catholics, adoption presented few difficulties.

Benjamin and his brothers were vaguely aware of the past events of their Irish heritage. They knew where their father Michael had been born and frequently, during the summertime, visited the Kerwin relatives in Shannon. They loved the farms and the wide-open spaces of the countryside

It was with much pride that Benjamin and his older brother Mike pursued their paper-route enterprise. They were endlessly willing to brag to their friends about their foray into this money-making, early-morning commitment. But the activity had a down side. It caused them both to be late for school on more than one occasion. All students who arrived at school in the morning after the start of classes were to report to the principal's office. No excuses were acceptable. There was an inevitable price to be paid for being late for school. On the morning of January 15th, both boys reported to the front office a full ten minutes after the morning bell.

"We can't have you two guys walking in late like this!" said hard-nosed Brother Francis, principal of St. Patrick's. "So what's your excuse this morning?"

"Our newspapers were delivered late again, Brother," said Mike.

"We're not going to take this. You cannot allow your paper route to disturb the routine of this school. This is the third time you have been late this month. We will not put up with this!"

Benjamin and Mike were given late slips that allowed them into their classes, and were told to report, after school, to the detention class.

Regrettably, the after-school detention fell on the same afternoon that Benjamin's Pee-Wee all-star team was to play the visiting St. George's School squad. Benjamin sat in the detention room with his brother and several other boys, all confined for various offences. Benjamin had looked forward to playing in this game, and sat, ruefully, tears easing down his cheeks. Young Brother Paul, who was on supervisory duty, soon noticed the distress on the face of Benjamin.

"Well, what is it, Benjamin?" he asked, bending down over the desk, his long black cassock chalk-stained about the sleeves.

"I'm supposed to be playing hockey against St. George's today," Benjamin replied, speaking just above a whisper.

"Oh? Well, you're already a little late for the game, aren't you?"

"I could still make it for the second and third period," suggested Benjamin, his teary eyes looking at Brother Paul.

"Well, lookit, Benjamin. I'll make a deal with you. You can go, but you'll have to come back here tomorrow afternoon and serve your time."

"Thank you, Brother Paul!" gushed Benjamin, his appreciation overflowing.

Benjamin could not believe his good luck. He quickly left the detention room, collected his hockey stick and skates from his own classroom, and went down to the school basement to put on his equipment.

Just as he had guessed, the first period of the game was ending as he got to his team's box at the rink.

"Why are you late, Kerwin?" asked Brother Henry, who was coaching.

"I had to go to detention, Brother," replied Benjamin.

The visiting St. George's team had scored early in the first period and St. Patrick's had been unable to even things up. On his first shift when the second period began, Benjamin felt nervous and clumsy as he skated. He played right wing and the action seemed to be so quickly paced that he hardly touched the puck. But then, on his second shift, he got hold of a loose puck at the opposition's blue line, skated in on the goalie, and shot wide of the net. But his centre man, Alan Kane, fought for the puck behind the net and sent it back out front where Benjamin whacked at it. The puck went in, tying the score.

The fans, standing on the high mounds of snow surrounding the rink, erupted into cheers. Even if this was only a game featuring eleven- and twelve-year-old boys, the interest in the contest had been very strong and scores of upper-level students had stayed after school to watch.

The remainder of the second period was a defensive struggle, with both teams trying to keep the puck out of their own end of the rink.

As the third and last period began, Benjamin was penalized for tripping, and while he was in the penalty box, the St. George's team came very close to going ahead, hitting the goal post once. But then, as Benjamin came out of the penalty box, he intercepted a pass from a St. George defenceman along the boards, skated in alone on their goalie, and beat him with a quick wrist shot.

His mates surrounded him, pummelling him in exaltation, some players coming off the bench to hug him. He fell to the ice, players on top of him. Then decorum was restored and the St. Patrick's team managed to hold off St. George's for the rest of the game. The final result was a 2-1 win for St. Patrick's.

It was a great moment for Benjamin. He'd been the hero of the contest and accolades from his teammates were relentless in the dressing room after the game. As he walked home with his brother Mike, the quiet celebratory mood continued.

"I saw your second goal just as I got out of detention," said Mike.

"Yeah, I was pretty lucky. The puck bounced right onto my stick just as I got out of the penalty box," marvelled Benjamin.

"God, you were skating really fast. Their defenceman was whacking at you from behind."

"I could feel him hitting my legs. But I was lucky I scored 'cause I wasn't sure where I was shooting the puck. Boy, was I nervous!"

They crunched toward home on the frozen sidewalks, Benjamin's hockey stick and skates and schoolbag slung over his shoulders.

It seemed that everyone at school had seen or heard about the game. The following day he was congratulated by many of the older boys from the high school grades on his stellar performance. After recess Mr. Shaw, his teacher, gave notice to his students that a hockey star was sitting in their midst.

"And not only is Benjamin a good hockey player, he's a fine student as well. So keep up the good work, Benjamin," said Mr. Shaw.

There was a smattering of applause from the grade five class.

Later that week, an after-school meeting was called by Brother Bonaventure, who was in charge of all the altar boys of the parish. This meeting was held in one of the classrooms of the high school section. Some students from most grades, from age ten and up, were altar boys.

Two houses of worship actually made up the parish of St. Patrick's, both very much in use. There was the old St. Patrick's Church which had been built in the 1830s to meet the needs of the growing number of Irish in the city. The parish also held services at the Diamond Harbour Chapel, which was located at Wolfe's Cove on the St. Lawrence riverside. Many Irish parishioners lived in the dock areas beside the river and worked on the wharves of the busy port.

Benjamin and Alan Kane served Mass at the old St. Patrick's Church, in the historic section of town, inside the walls of the old city. It was an imposing structure with a high steeple that at one time had dominated the skyline of that old city section. They would meet at the venerable St. John's Gate and walk to the church together. They always entered the church complex through a small back door, which the caretaker, Mr. O'Leary, kept open for the priest who was to say the Mass. Mr. O'Leary actually lived in a small apartment which could be reached from the sacristy. He was employed as a full-time caretaker by the church.

Benjamin and Alan would put on their soutanes and surplices in the sacristy, the large room behind the altar with elaborate commodes full of Mass vestments, albs, and other linens. The sacristy also stored the sacred utensils.

Benjamin's religion was an ever-present feature of his youth, both at home and with his Irish-Catholic community. His parents made certain that the children in the family attended Mass on Sundays and Holy Days. They said the family rosary, knees on the floor, as part of their daily routine after supper in the evenings.

Most students attending school during the Second World War years were similar in their spiritual attitudes. They considered themselves to be close to God and responsible for their behaviour. Conscience was a constant companion, if not a friend. Fear was a real determinant in their lives. Families in financial trouble did not have reliable support systems. It took teamwork to keep things together. Families prayed to God to deliver them from difficulty, from sickness, from unemployment, from hunger. Churches were filled with praying people who believed their fears were justified and who carried a religious and social consciousness around with them.

Benjamin Kerwin was sensitive to the concerns of his parents about the health and well-being of their children. He also read the newspaper headlines every morning as he delivered the dailies to his customers.

"Mike," he asked his brother one morning, as they trudged along the snowy streets, "how long will the war last?"

"Nobody knows," Mike answered, looking wise. "Maybe by the summer holidays." He stopped to pull a newspaper out of the bundle. "Do you have a hockey practice tonight?"

Benjamin didn't think about the war much, however; he lived for his skating and his hockey games and his good times with Alan Kane and getting his homework done and, again, whether he would be able to score some more goals in the next hockey game. Although he got himself into the odd bit of mischief, he did not look for it, nor was he known as a trouble maker.

So when he entered the classroom for the altar boys meeting, he was somewhat surprised when Brother Bonaventure called on him and Alan Kane to stand at the front of the classroom. He was at a loss to understand why he would be singled out.

There were at least forty boys assembled at the meeting, students from grade four to grade twelve. These were the boys who got up early on winter mornings, as well as the rest of the year, to serve Mass. They were considered to be the "cream of the crop" among the students of St. Patrick's.

"Tell me, Benjamin," began Brother Bonaventure, "how long have you been serving Mass?"

The students were rapt with attention.

"Almost one year, Brother," answered Benjamin.

"And you, Alan?" continued Brother Bonaventure.

"We started together, Brother," said Alan.

"Now, Benjamin. How long did it take you to learn the Latin answers required to be an altar boy?"

"I'm not sure, Brother. I think it took a few weeks."

"It took you ten days, Benjamin. I distinctly remember. At the time we all were very surprised that you had learned the responses so quickly."

Benjamin took a deep breath and looked at Alan, a slight grin on his face. But the ominous silence after Brother Bonaventure had spoken worried him.

"However," continued Brother Bonaventure, "it has come to our attention that some disrespect for the Holy Sacrifice of the Mass has been demonstrated by one of these altar boys."

He looked at both Benjamin and Alan Kane, his eyes moving back and forth between the two boys. He was a tall, red-faced man with a reputation as a tough disciplinarian who would put up with no nonsense.

"Which one of you helped Father Doyle serve communion last week?" he asked.

One of the duties of an altar boy was to hold a gold-coloured plate under the chin of the Communion recipient who knelt at the Communion rail, so that if the host accidentally fell from the priest's fingers, it would not fall to the floor of the church.

Benjamin and Alan had served Mass for the previous weekly period, and Benjamin had been the one who had assisted the priest during the distribution of Holy Communion.

"I did, Brother," answered Benjamin.

"Well. We have had a serious complaint from a parishioner that you were intentionally hitting people on the chin with the edge of the plate. Is this true, Benjamin?"

Benjamin knew that this could happen. On some occasions he had inadvertently nudged the chin or mouth area of a Communion recipient. But he had never done this intentionally. At times, some of the priests who gave out Communion did so at a pretty fast tempo and it was not always possible for altar boys to keep up with them. It took some skill to avoid hitting a person's chin.

"I never did that on purpose, Brother," said Benjamin.

"It is my solemn duty to inform you, Benjamin, that your services as an altar boy are no longer required. We're sorry about this. At one time, you showed a lot of promise. You can leave now. We have other things to discuss, and since you will no longer be serving, you can go. We cannot have people who show a mockery for the Holy Sacrifice of the Mass."

Benjamin left the classroom in a daze. He could not understand what was happening. He thought back on his behaviour with Alan down at the church sacristy. They had laughed about a lot of things. They laughed about their soutanes, and sometimes pranced around pretending the soutanes were dresses. They laughed at some of the people who came to church dressed in weird outfits, or who stuck their tongues out really far when they received Communion. They sometimes went into Mr. O'Leary's apartment just off the sacristy and snickered at his corny jokes. But Benjamin could not remember showing disrespect during the services he took part in relating to the Holy Sacrifice of the Mass, and the Benediction rituals he sometimes served.

He walked home, devastated at what had occurred. How would he explain this to his mom and dad when they found out? And they surely would, in time. He enjoyed serving Mass. It was something he shared with Alan and some of the other guys. Soon everyone would know that he had been expelled from serving Mass.

He lay in his bed wondering how this had happened. He would speak to Father Enright about it. Father Enright knew him well, and knew that he was a good altar boy.

Benjamin was up early the next morning, delivering the newspapers with Mike.

"So what's this about you getting thrown off the altar, Ben?" said Mike, as they slid down an ice-covered, hilly sidewalk.

"I don't know. I don't understand what happened," answered Benjamin.

"Aw, don't worry about it," his brother reassured him. "Now you can help me with my paper route all the time. But we gotta speed it up. We don't wanna be late for school."

Aunt Emily

BENJAMIN KERWIN'S Aunt Emily took up residence at the family's flat while she was working at the hotel. She was his father's sister who had not married. Evidently she did not enjoy living by herself in a rented room, having been accustomed to a close familial environment. She'd been raised in the farming community of Shannon, north of Quebec City, just as Michael had been. She was a Kerwin through and through—proud of her Irish heritage and pious in her religious beliefs.

In exchange for squeezing into an already crowded situation, Aunt Emily helped to keep the Kerwin family afloat by contributing part of her salary. A single bed was inserted into one corner of the boys' room for her, and under these spartan conditions she slept for many a year.

It was only natural that Emily Kerwin would seek employment in the capital city as she grew into adulthood. She, Michael, and their three other siblings had been educated at the small Shannon country school which terminated at the grade six level. The eldest brother, Willie, had started running the family farm after their parents had passed away. It was incumbent upon the other siblings to pursue opportunities elsewhere.

Aunt Emily was up early six days a week and walked to her job at the hotel. She worked in the main kitchen preparing both room service and dining room fare.

21

Although she was not a chef and did not concoct main dishes, she did help the cooks in baking desserts and performing ancillary tasks.

Originally, Emily Kerwin had been hired as a chambermaid, one of the positions in the hotel that young, single working girls aspired to secure. There was a certain measure of pride attached to this occupation, the Château Frontenac Hotel being world-renowned. The management of the hotel sought to encourage and maintain the virginal status of its chambermaids, and the momentous decision by a chambermaid to marry often meant the loss of this employment. In Emily's case, she had simply decided, after working the rooms for a number of years, to replace a person in the kitchen who had retired, having been made aware of the opening through a friendship she had struck up with one of the kitchen staff.

As a single woman approaching middle age, Emily Kerwin was modest to a fault, a trait that weighed upon the Kerwin boys from time to time. She would sometimes lock the bedroom door during the evenings while she "went about her business." This the boys considered to be usurpation, and when it occurred one of them would stand up on the toilet seat next to the bedroom and peek through the small inner window—installed to enhance air circulation but usually kept closed—to see what was going on. The glazed glass of the square ventilator revealed an imperfect view of their aunt's activities. Sometimes she would be trying on clothes and looking at herself in the dresser mirror, and sometimes kneeling by her small bed, praying the rosary.

The older boys tended to regard her with a tinge of flippancy because of her piousness. The wall space surrounding her bed was covered with iconic images of several saints, as well as a large colour print of Our Lady of Perpetual Help. She would often walk around the house with rosary beads wrapped around a clenched hand, and often seemed to be in prayer when she wasn't talking.

The younger children, however, enjoyed her presence. Aunt Emily, when she arrived home from work early, would bring sweets from her favourite bakery—Hetherington's. She would bounce into the kitchen with the daintily wrapped white boxes and place them on the table where the girls would expectantly gather around to watch her untie the strings and open the containers, to reveal an assortment of honey doughnuts, mille feuilles, and éclairs.

While Rosalie, Benjamin's mother, could see the benefits of the additional income, Emily's presence in her home was something she never fully accepted. Rosalie's sister-in-law did not speak a word of French, nor did she ever have a mind to do so. Conversely, Emily tended to treat her brother's wife as a stranger who had married into the Kerwin clan, and as a woman who had shown irresponsible control over her fecundity, being the mother of six children.

Little genuine communication was interchanged between the two women. Yet, surprisingly, the antipathy seldom rose to the surface. After all, Emily was absent from the house most of the time—at the hotel six days a week and frequently visiting her acquaintances after work, arriving home late in the evening. She ate at the hotel in the employees' cafeteria for the most part, and therefore was usually absent from the Kerwin dinner table.

However, a few days preceding a religious festival such as Christmas, Easter, or St. Patrick's Day, Aunt

Emily would commandeer the kitchen and go about what was, for the Kerwin children, the forever memorable process of "the baking of the loaf." In this endeavour she would use mountainous quantities of flour, raisins, and other ingredients, and cover the kitchen table with a rolling mass of dough, which she then laboriously mauled and mutilated until it was a compact, ominous hulk. The behemoth was then hauled into an enormous cast iron pot designed specifically for the occasion.

As the loaf began to bake in the oven, the entire flat and its stairway were filled with a sweet-smelling aroma.

Many hours later, Aunt Emily would cautiously open the oven door and, wearing two oven mitts, skid the black pot out and remove the cover. She would then take an ordinary kitchen fork and probe, first the surface, then deeply into the middle of the loaf. If she was satisfied that the baking process was sufficient, the cooling period would begin. Eventually, she would remove the loaf from the pot and wrap it in cloth.

It was not until the next day that the family was permitted to test the result of this monumental undertaking. What came off in solid perfect slices was a dark brown piece of goodness full of moist raisins and currants and dates. Since it was such a large cake, it lasted many days, and it tasted more and more delicious until the last morsel had disappeared.

As a young woman, Emily was tall and attractively slim. When the Kerwin children looked at photographs of Emily—pictures taken as she turned twenty years of age—they were deeply impressed. The older Kerwin boys speculated on why she had not gotten married, and finally decided that she was too pure and too religious to have submitted to the intimate ramifications of the married state.

Benjamin looked upon his Aunt Emily as a bene-
factor for the growing family, a generous woman who
was a welcome sight whenever she appeared. He would
gaze at one particular picture of her in a family album, a
young woman staring off to one side, clear-eyed, and
with the start of a smile on her face. She was wrapped in
a dark satiny dress with a tight collar that rose to just
beneath her chin. Her hair, pressed down close to her
head in shiny waves, was parted in the middle and,
although it was not evident from the picture, he imag-
ined it to be tied up in the back in a ponytail. This
picture, which he loved the most, was taken in the 1920s
and he thought that in it Aunt Emily looked like one of
the actresses from *Gone with the Wind*.

Emily attended services at St. Patrick's Church as
often as she could, considering the demands of her job.
In addition to this, she was forever counselling the
Kerwin children as to the benefits of exemplary behaviour, and advising them to go to church frequently, and
to pray the rosary.

On occasion, Emily would take one of the younger
children to an evening religious service, likely a regular
Tuesday devotion to Our Mother of Perpetual Help.
When the liturgy was over, they would stroll leisurely up
La rue St. Jean, one of the main commercial streets of
Quebec, and drop into her choice restaurant. Aunt Emily
usually opted to sit on one of the chrome stools at the
lunch counter where they would order two banana splits
with heaps of ice cream and fruit slices covered with a
chocolate syrup.

If Benjamin was the fortunate child to be chosen for
this religion-and-restaurant tour, he was more than willing to submit to Aunt Emily's caprices. He would sit on

the stool, his legs dangling, copiously shovelling in the sweetness of the moment, and marvelling at the blend of massive wall mirrors and neon lighting of the bustling public eatery.

Sometimes, in the silence of night, a shrill call would emanate from the corner in which Emily's bed was located. She would summon up the saints by name, and the Blessed Virgin Mary, and the three boys in the room would awaken and sit up. One of them, likely Joseph, the eldest, would go to Aunt Emily's bedside to tend to her, inquiring sleepily what the difficulty was. Her cries usually meant that she was in the throes of an attack of leg cramps, one of her calf muscles having curled into a hard ball.

She would eventually sit up at the side of her cot, pouring out a continuous incantation to Saint Jude or Saint Francis, and Joseph would bend down and massage her leg until the muscle had relaxed and the pain subsided. She would then move on to prayers of thanksgiving for the pain relieved and the suffering endured.

Benjamin, from his sofa out in the hallway, would always be awakened by the episode and accepted it as just another part of Aunt Emily's eccentricity.

The Kerwins lived on Rue St. Joachim in a French-speaking neighbourhood in which most of the people were working class and lived in rented accommodations, many of which were flats with long inside stairwells. It was a city of landlords and tenants. A lot of the houses were three-storey structures with A-frame roofs, jammed together along the old streets like European-style row houses. Very few of them had a front lawn to speak of. In some cases a small back yard held a minute vegetable garden, a revelation in the brief summer season. The older section of the city was built on a hill with dozens of streets running up and down and thousands of houses ingeniously crafted to cope with the slanting topography.

Anglophone families were few and far between in the old city, even though some sectors of town had a higher proportion of English speakers.

When Rosalie, Benjamin's mother, had moved to Quebec City with her husband Michael a few years after their marriage, she had relinquished close family ties to her siblings who were making their living in the area of Lac St. Jean. But they did come to Quebec City and visited Rosalie with some frequency.

Rosalie did not hide her culture from her children, although she practised her English unceasingly. Her favourite radio programs were on the French stations, so the Kerwin children listened to the daily serials as they grew up. Rosalie's intermittent bouts of frustration regarding the behaviour of her offspring would be expressed wholly in the language of Lac St. Jean. She had emerged from a warm culture which had produced a gregarious group of brothers and sisters who, because of their visits, left an unerasable mark on the Kerwin children.

Because of this Gallic influence in their lives, the children of Michael Kerwin considered themselves to be propitiously bicultural. The friendships that the children made with neighbourhood kids also helped to instill in them an ability to get along quite adequately in French.

Although Emily Kerwin lived in a city which was the old capital of French North America, overwhelmingly populated by francophones, she did not see it as a necessity to blend into the other culture. She worked for a hotel that was owned and operated by an English-speaking institution –Canadian Pacific Railways. Most of the managerial positions at the hotel were held by English-speaking men. She had been reared by the descendants of immigrants from Ireland, a clannish people who spoke English in their own way and lived independently simple agricultural lives.

Across the street from the Kerwin residence was a rather large complex where priests and older students lived. Most of these men were attending courses or teaching at the Grand Seminaire attached to Laval University, and used the complex as a dorm. As well as single rooms, the building contained a dining room that was run by an order of Sisters who had their own sleeping quarters on site. There was also a chapel area with several altars in small alcoves where daily Mass was said by many of the priests in residence. This property also had a tennis court and a spacious vacant lot used by the Sisters for walking and gardening.

The Kerwin boys frequently served Mass for the priests in the chapel across the street, and also cultivated friendships with the seminary students. During the summertimes, several of the rooms were occupied by American priests and students who studied French at Laval University. The Americans seemed surprised that an English-speaking family would be living in the old city. They had expected a complete immersion into the French culture, but when they heard the children of Michael Kerwin calling to each other in the street, they were struck by what they considered an anomaly. The conversations they initiated often resulted in lasting friendships.

Benjamin would frequently roam through the hallways of the dorm and knock on the door of one of the priests' rooms. He got to know many of them and would sit and talk and listen to radio programs with them. Benjamin held most of these American priests in very high regard, and after they had returned to the United States he exchanged correspondence with several of them.

It was at the complex across the street where Benjamin made the acquaintance of Gilbert Tremblay, who was the custodian and a jack-of-all-trades. He was a stocky, middle-aged bachelor with a ready smile and a dry sense of humour. Benjamin would visit him and Gilbert would allow the boy to accompany him through the building where repairs had to be completed on a regular basis. He loved to practise his English with Benjamin, who would be helpful in handing tools to Gilbert taken from the tool kit, and doing other small tasks. During such times Benjamin became aware of Gilbert's interest in Aunt Emily.

Gilbert Tremblay had already spoken on many occasions to Rosalie, Benjamin's mother. On hot summer evenings, Rosalie would sometimes sit at the open window that overlooked the street and allow whatever breeze there was to cool the front living room. Gilbert would cross the street and station himself just below Rosalie's window.

They would chat like old acquaintances for a spell, Gilbert revealing to Rosalie that he hailed from the Montmagny area south of Quebec City where he'd been raised with ten siblings on a dairy farm. He would assure Rosalie of the fine behaviour of her son Benjamin, and what a good lad he was. Gilbert would also make subtly placed inquiries about Emily Kerwin, questions about her employment and past history. Rosalie assured Gilbert that Emily had never married and at the present time seemed to be content with her lot in life working at the hotel, going to church, and spending time with her single lady friends.

Gilbert Tremblay's room faced the Kerwin flat across the street and since he rose early every morning to begin his chores at the students' residence, he would always see Emily Kerwin emerge from the Kerwin doorway heading off to her work at the hotel. He saw her as a tallish, attractive woman and wondered how he could get to know her better. He was aware, with information gathered from Benjamin, that Emily did not speak much French, but that was fine with him as he loved to speak English. He listened to English radio all the time, and read *Time* magazine and other English publications. He had said hello to her, calling out across the street on a few occasions as she entered the flat. She had not seemed to respond very enthusiastically, but that did not discourage him.

One cool September Saturday evening there was a knock on the door of the Kerwin flat, made as the family was in the midst of the saying of the family rosary. All were on their knees, gathered around the kitchen area. There was no pause in the recital of the Joyful Mysteries and the Our Fathers and the Hail Marys and the Glory Be to the Fathers as one of the girls answered the door and allowed Gilbert Tremblay to enter. He promptly knelt down and willingly joined in to the remainder of the recitation, which culminated with the Hail Holy Queen, Mother of Mercy.

As the prayers ended, all rose to their feet and looked at Gilbert. He was holding a small bouquet of yellow flowers and stood awkwardly, with a small grimace on his face. He then gave the flowers to Rosalie, saying that they were from the Sisters' garden in the vacant lot of the residence. A couple of the boys snickered as this initial statement was made, for they knew why Gilbert had made this visit, but they soon lost interest in this bit of curiosity and quickly went outside to play some street hockey.

The entire Kerwin family, including Aunt Emily, was present this Saturday evening. It was a good time for Michael, the eve of his weekly Sunday holiday from work, and a period when he was pleased with the world and his growing family. After listening to some small talk, in French, between Rosalie and Gilbert, mostly about the weather, and before any onset of awkwardness, he suggested that they sit down at the kitchen table and have a game of euchre—a card game where each player is dealt five cards and the team naming the trump must win three hands to earn a point. This card game was very popular with farm families of Irish descent, and both Michael and Emily had fond memories of many table-thumping nights as they grew up, when neighbouring farm families would visit and play a rousing game of euchre.

So on this evening Aunt Emily teamed up with Michael against Rosalie and Gilbert. Since Gilbert was not too familiar with the game of euchre, he had to be reminded about the rules on several occasions during the evening.

And since the game requires the full attention of the participant, there was little time for talk other than what had to do with the game. Still, Rosalie noticed how Gilbert sneaked glimpses at Emily during the evening, and how Emily seldom looked at Gilbert.

Yet the evening was a success, and the boys came into the house after their street hockey session and listened to the radio broadcast of the Montreal Canadiens–Boston Bruins game from the Montreal Forum, and the girls were busy with their activities, and it was past eleven o'clock before the euchre game ended and Gilbert left the flat.

If Emily Kerwin was aware of the special attention bestowed on her by Gilbert Tremblay, she did not let on. It was as if she was immune to such courtesies. There seemed to be not a scintilla of flirtatious reckoning in her make-up. Even if Aunt Emily was a woman of limited financial means, she was fiercely independent, and seemed to need no one to make her feel complete.

It was not unusual to see inter-cultural weddings in the old city. Many of the school friends of the Kerwin boys had francophone mothers or fathers. Since most of the Irish descendants of the immigrants and francophone inhabitants of Quebec were Roman Catholic, marriages between the two groups presented few problems. The family of Michael and Rosalie Kerwin was an example of how two languages and cultures could come together and produce accommodation and solidarity.

Gilbert Tremblay did not flag in his interest in Emily Kerwin after the euchre game, even if he felt that she had demonstrated a sort of indifference toward him. Several days after the evening spent at the Kerwins, he intercepted Emily as she came up the street on her way home. He had stood on the sidewalk pretending to work on the doorway of the students' house until he saw her at a distance and crossed the street to confront her. After mutual words of greeting, she grasped the door handle, seemingly eager to go into the house. Gilbert quickly asked Emily if she would be interested in going out to dinner with him to a restaurant in the near future. She brusquely responded with a "No, thank you" and escaped into the stairway of the flat.

Such a rebuff was somewhat humiliating to Gilbert, his fantasies about being with her destroyed in one swoop.

Yet he did not take out his frustration on Benjamin. They continued to be good friends and the boy still tagged along with Gilbert on his rounds, as they bantered on in English about the hockey stars on the Montreal Canadiens, especially Maurice "Rocket" Richard, held in great esteem by both of them.

Emily Kerwin, dedicated in chaste observance to her job at the hotel and to her church and to her "family," the children of Michael Kerwin, resisted any temptation, if ever there was one, to submit to the admonition of anyone, and persisted in her absolute sense of independence.

A Day in the Life

JACK MILLER knocked on the screen door of the farm-house. He did not wait for an answer but entered and walked into the large kitchen area. He stopped in the middle of the room and wiped the dust from his glasses with a crumpled cloth handkerchief until he spied the newspapers in their usual place on a small corner table. He went over and rustled through them, chose one of recent date, and then sat at the broad bare wooden table, spreading the latest news before him, immediately absorbed.

By the time Tom Slavin came in from the stable with a pail of freshly drawn milk, he sensed that the house had been invaded, albeit by friendly forces. He'd heard the screen door slam while he was hand milking the cow, Moll, and felt it could only be Jack. Tom's wife, Marg, had driven to the railway station to pick up the mail and she could not be back so soon.

"Lovely morning, Jack. You're early," Tom said, loud and lyrical.

Jack Miller was quite deaf and paid no heed to Tom. His head was bent, his nose almost touching the news-paper. The early summer sun streamed through the window by the kitchen table. If the brilliant light made reading easier, it also prevented old Jack from noticing any peripheral movement around him.

This visit was a weekly ritual and had gone on for a number of years. Jack Miller had little to say now, being well into his eighties. Still, apart from his deafness, he was still strong in the legs and could be seen walking the dirt roads of Shannon, a lonely black-suited figure with the inevitable white straw hat. He had farmed up on the rock-strewn hillside of the 6th range most of his life, eking out an existence with his chickens and turkeys, horses and cattle. Now one of his sons was running things, even though the son also worked at the nearby Valcartier Military Camp.

Why Jack had never bothered to subscribe to a newspaper, Tom could not understand. When Jack did speak about events, though, he seemed to be well informed, and demonstrated an astute, if not very verbose, opinion.

Tom finally got Jack's attention by placing the butter churn at one end of the table, where Marg would later use the creamy milk to make the butter.

"The Americans have got their hands full with the airlift, I see," observed Jack.

"Yes, sir," agreed Tom, speaking just below a yell, "that Harry Truman is a tough little son-of-a-bitch."

"What's that?"

"Harry Truman!" Tom said, leaning close to Jack's ear.

"Ah, yes. The haberdasher from Missouri," said Jack.

Old Jack laughed then, quietly, and took a pipe from his suit-coat pocket, found a pack of Rose Quesnel pipe tobacco in another pocket, and began a routine which would soon have him happily sucking in the acridly flavoured smoke with glazed eyes.

It was late June of 1948, and the two boys of Marg and Tom Slavin had been free of the schoolhouse for a week now. They had already done their chores in the stable, had gathered the eggs from the hen house, and were already on the road this sun-soaked morning with their fishing poles, fashioned from carefully chosen tree limbs. They'd also dug up dozens of fleshy worms from in and around the manure pile behind the barn, tucked them into a tin can, then headed off, gently, before their father could think up more jobs for them.

Hughie and Patrick Slavin were twelve and eleven years of age, respectively.

The coming summer days offered the opportunity to spend a lot of time with other farm boys, fishing for speckled trout in the various brooks flowing into the Rivière aux Pins. They would walk for miles from early morn, up and down the sandy roads where the infrequent passing of a car would set off a miniature dust storm, searching for a specific spot mentioned by some grown-up as the ideal location. Then they'd unsheathe their crude fishing rods, fitted with white string and hook. Sitting along the edge of a brook, the rods baited with the fat reddish worms, they'd wait for the thrill of a bite, slapping at the horse flies and mosquitoes that pestered them.

In the afternoons, they might play war games on the rocky hills along the 6th range, a long narrow trail threading its way past the farms and homesteads of Irish descendants of settlers who came to Canada as far back as the 1820s. The distant staccato of machine-gun fire from the Valcartier Military Camp lent credibility to their inane activities. Or they might decide to raid an onion patch on one of the farms, eating the raw onions in a strange fit of rapacity. Tom and Marg could easily tell if their boys had been to the onion patch, their breaths on these occasions being an assault on the senses.

Just the week before, a few days into their summer break, as they had trudged along a dirt road with their lunches and fishing branches, a car had pulled up from behind the Slavin brothers. It was their older cousin Michael, son of their Uncle Joe from Montreal. Michael was a salesman who owned a summer cottage along the Riviere aux Pins in Shannon. He was also a Royal Canadian Air Force veteran, large and athletic. They knew and admired him from his memorable, though infrequent, visits to their home.

"Where you headed for?" he bellowed at the boys over the drone of the car motor.

"Just up to the stream behind Martin Bowles's place," Hughie called out.

"Well, get in. I'll be going past there," Michael commanded.

Once in the back seat of the car, an impressive-looking sedan with leather upholstery, they felt honoured to be with this Second World War hero and baseball pitcher.

"Let me tell you, boys," he was saying then, powering up the narrow winding road, "I'd give anything in the world to change places with you today. You're just young guys. It's a beautiful day in the country. Have you any idea how lucky you are? I'd sooner have what you have today than anything else in the world."

He dropped them off at the designated spot, wished them good luck, and sped off in the usual cloud of dust.

Both Hughie and Patrick knew they would never

forget that brief ride and the effusive expressions of their older cousin.

* * *

Old Jack Miller crossed one leg over the other and drew in the aroma of Rose Quesnel tobacco smoke. Tom Slavin, now in his mid-forties, did not smoke himself, but he did rather enjoy the smell of pipe tobacco. Little extended conversation occurred during one of Jack's visits. Whether it was the strain of speaking loud or just the lack of topics for discussion, neither man bothered to analyze. Although Tom had work to do, he would nonetheless sit with Jack for a half-hour or so accepting the silence between them as part of the visit.

But soon Tom could make out the sound of an automobile engine and on this morning his wife Marg pulled into the yard and was soon at the screen door with a canvas mailbag slung over her shoulder.

The Slavins ran the Post Office in the community. They picked up the mail daily at the railway station. Elmer King would drop in every weekday evening, and deliver the mail to the farms along a circular route of approximately 25 miles. He'd also pick up outgoing letters and packages which Tom or Marg would deliver to the railway mail car the following day. These routines were close to sacred at a time when the Post Office ran the only meaningful form of communication of the written word.

Marg set the mail bag on the floor beside the door and smiled at Jack.

"And how are you this beautiful day, Jack?" she said.

"I'm fine, thank you," responded Jack, sitting up in his chair.

Tom observed that in Jack's conversations with Marg, the deaf man always seemed to understand what Marg was saying. She seldom raised her voice nor repeated herself while talking to him. It was as if he was then not a deaf old man at all but a man with the full power of his faculties, vital and alert. She was a beautiful petite woman in the full bloom of life, this day wearing a knee-length blue skirt and a white blouse. A free flow of light brown hair fell across her shoulders. They'd all said that on the day Tom married Marg, he'd won the top prize—the Irish Sweepstakes.

"And where are the two brats? I don't see them around," she said to Tom.

"Ah, they're gone for the day," said Tom, waving an arm, a little sarcasm in his voice.

"You know, I want them to work on the garden. The bugs are eating up the leaves. Bugs bad in your garden this year, Jack?"

"Yes, Marg. I think we've got the Baltimore beetle this year."

"Oh, yes? Well, they're real critters."

When the boys made themselves available, Marg would give them glass jars to pick the dreaded potato beetles off the leaves of the plants. She tended to be responsible for the health of the vegetables, especially at this time of the year when the little black and red devils were ravenous and at their peak. The land was favourable to root vegetables, so the generations of Slavins, since emigrating from Ireland in 1824, had traditionally planted lots of potatoes, carrots, turnips, and beets. When harvested, most were stored in the cellar below the kitchen, a cool satisfactory niche during the icy Quebec winters.

"Let them have their fun today," said Tom. "We'll nail them tomorrow."

As June turned into July, the hay would have to be cut, gathered, and piled in the barn. Tom had already used his sons' help in this yearly task for several years now. They enjoyed tramping down the hay, perched rather perilously atop the loaded hay wagon, as Tom would pitchfork up timothy, the grain that served as part of the winter diet for the cows and horses. Then the old mare, Belle, who was twenty-five years old if she was a day, would pull the wagon across the bumpy fields, the boys hanging on to one of the slats in the framework of the wagon, high above the ground, the load wobbling and pitching. The boys loved this "work" and laughed and giggled as the mare made her languorous trek back to the barn. On such occasions Tom would usually sit at the front of the wagon, also seated high, using the long reins to guide old Belle. He'd frequently half turn to warn the boys to hang on and be careful. On such days as these, he'd lapse into a dreamy state, thanking the heavens for his good luck.

* * *

Walking in the midst of a copse of young spruce and balsam, the two boys, Hughie and Patrick, soon could make out the sound of the brook they had fished once before. This rill ran through the property of Martin Bowles, whose acreage lay to the north of Tom Slavin's farm. It was understood among the Irish families that the boys could roam these areas, so they felt comfortable setting up on the mossy banks of the brook. It was a suitable spot filled with surrounding young trees, but not bereft of the usual brambles and inescapable mosquitoes.

After just a few moments of sitting in the tranquil sheen of the sun's rays, Patrick spotted, imbedded in the water on the opposite side of the brook, a brown jute bag. Hughie, his curiosity challenged, removed his running shoes and socks and waded across the six-foot stretch of chilly running water to investigate. What the bag could contain mystified both of them, and when Hughie lifted it from the water it seemed inexplicably, ominously heavy for his 12-year-old arms. Yet he soon managed to untie the cord that secured its contents. He hoisted the bag up high to pour out its secret—a drowned cat.

They were both momentarily stunned.

"You know, I knew it was a cat," said Hughie.

"Paddy Sheehey said he was gonna drown a cat up here. He told me during class," observed Patrick.

"Yeah, he's a cruel little bastard."

"We should bury it up here somewhere," suggested Patrick, pointing back to the trees.

"Yeah. Better than leaving it in the water to rot."

Hughie leaned down and picked up the dead cat by the tail. It was a largely white carcass, with black markings.

They used some stout branches that they found lying about and managed to scoop out a hole a few feet deep. Patrick clawed at the earth with his bare hands to deepen it more.

"You think that's deep enough?"

"Yeah, that's okay."

Hughie nudged the cat into the crevice with his foot. It fell with a dull thud, and they immediately kicked the loose earth over the carcass.

It was a hot, humid day already, and with their quickened breathing from the work of digging, they stood over the small grave, the full throbbing sound of summer filling their ears.

"I don't think we should fish around here," said Hughie.

"Maybe we could follow the brook upstream a little," offered Patrick.

They soon were fighting their way through the growth, trying to avoid the sharp branches and swatting at the flies. At one point, they began to hear, above the cacophony of insect noise, a strange buzzing sensation. They could not tell from which direction it came at first, but soon they were attracted to a small clearing on their side of the running water. In the centre of this small open area, they could make out a flurry of voluminous insect activity. As they approached this phenomenon, they were startled to see that the multitude of insects were feeding upon the remains of a white horse.

"God, is that Belle?" exclaimed Patrick.

"It sure looks like her," said Hughie, somberly.

A few weeks before, their old mare, Belle, had wandered off the farm with the melting snow, and had disappeared. How she had managed to get through the fencing, nobody knew.

Inquiries had been made for several days as to the whereabouts of their oldest mare. The general area surrounding the farm had been searched, without success. Now the boys could not wait to get home to inform their dad and mother as to what they'd found.

So they abandoned their fishing plans for that day, scrambled back along the edge of the brook to the road, and half-walked, half-ran the several miles back to the farm.

Out of breath, Hughie was the first to burst into the house, to find his mother working the butter churn at the kitchen table. Jack Miller sat in one corner of the kitchen rocking back and forth. The aroma of tobacco filled the room.

"We found Belle! Mom! We found Belle up near the Bowles's place!"

Hughie could hardly contain himself.

"No! You didn't!" responded Marg.

She stopped the churn and took Joseph by the shoulders.

Jack Miller stopped the rocker.

"She's dead! She's lying up in the bush! The insects are eating her!"

"Oh, my God!" cried Marg, and pulled her son close to her, hugging him. "And where's Patrick?"

"He's looking for Dad."

"Your Dad's over in the field working on the fences."

Hughie began to cry, suddenly, tears gushing down his cheeks.

Marg held him tightly.

"But she was an old, old lady, Hughie. We sort of felt that she must have died somewhere."

"But she was so good . . . and so friendly," whimpered Hughie.

"Yes, you're so right," coddled Marg.

"Mom, it was so disgusting!"

"I know, son. But that's where most of the animals die, in the woods. And the insects and the maggots finish them off and soon there's only bones left. I'm sorry you had to see it, but that's life."

Hughie's body felt lean and hard and sinewy to her. He didn't allow himself to be held closely very often. He was a mite taller than his mom now, but she realized how the child in him was still there. He wiped his tears aside with a soiled hand, smearing his tanned cheeks.

"Here, Hughie. Let me wipe this off."

She released him and quickly took a washcloth from a drawer, dipped it in cool basin water, and cleaned his face.

For the first time, Hughie then noticed Jack Miller in the corner of the room.

"Good day, Mr. Miller," he said, composing himself now. "We found our old mare Belle up in the bush this morning."

"Yes, Hughie. So I heard you say. You know, we lost a few horses over the years that way. Sometimes they just get old and act sort of crazy," offered Jack.

"I'm going out to find Dad, Mom," Hughie said suddenly.

"Yes, Hughie. Go tell your Dad. I have to finish up here."

The boys spent the afternoon scraping potato bugs from the leaves of the potato plants. They had to fill a good-sized pickle jar with them. The chore was back-bending and boring. The also plucked some weeds from around other vegetable plants, working into the heat of this late June afternoon.

"Shall we tell Dad about the cat?" said Patrick, standing, stretching his arms out.

"Naw, we don't have to talk about it," judged his older brother.

"Why do you think Paddy would want to drown a cat?"

"We're not sure it was him."

"Well, he told us at school he was gonna do it."

"He's a moron to begin with."

"You think he saw somebody else do it?"

"Probably."

The artillery shells from the Valcartier Military Camp began firing then. Thunderous blasts echoed across the tall fir trees and then the resultant spume of smoke could be seen on the large scar of the distant Pinkney's mountain.

The boys stood up in the vegetable patch and looked into the distance.

"See that, Paddy," said Joseph, "the sound is slower to travel, so we see the smoke, then we hear the crash."

"Yeah."

And when the evening settled in, after supper, the boys sat on the steps leading up to the porch, listening to the call of the bullfrogs from the nearby swampy bogs.

For just a few months now, the people of Shannon were experiencing a change in their lives—the arrival of electric power in their homes. The workers from the Quebec Power Company had installed the wiring on poles along the sandy roads. Up to 1948, the citizens had depended on coal-oil lamps for night light. Few families on these farms had indoor plumbing. Water requirements were provided usually by the use of a hand pump in the kitchen, the water raised from wells below the farmhouses.

One feature that the farms did have was the telephone with its early party lines.

As the evening darkened, Hughie and Patrick could see the distant sparkle of a few lights from the military camp, the border of which began at the edge of Tom Slavin's farm.

But on this moonless night, the sky was truly darkening, and soon the massive open panorama would reveal the multitudes of stars to them. They loved to watch the heavens at night, especially during summertime. For, interlaced in the colossal outness beat the pulse of God's majesty—endlessness. Sometimes they would lie on the grass outside the house at night with just the dim light of the solitary electric bulb from their kitchen window behind them. They'd marvel at the racing of the "falling stars" and the dancing luminous colours of the northern lights. Patrick, amazingly, would often fall asleep. Hughie would awaken him, pushing him with his foot, and tell him to go to bed.

Alphonsus

HE EDGED THROUGH the tavern doorway, a temporary winter two-door system that was difficult to manipulate, and stepped out into the midnight air. It felt fresh; large snowflakes fell on his glasses. Echoes of laughter reverberated inside the tavern.

Alphonsus Kerwin put his thumb and forefinger into his mouth and issued forth a powerful, piercing whistle, a style of summons he was still willing to use in his thirty-seventh year. For support, he hung onto the bus stop post until a compact dark taxi sidled up to him along the curb. He pulled the door open and literally fell into the front seat of the car.

"Champlain Street! 29 Champlain!" he commanded.

"Oui, Monsieur."

The taxi driver quickly looked at Alphonsus, knowingly, cheerfully, having driven him to Champlain Street a few times before.

"You, sir!" began Alphonsus, "surely remember Jack Kennedy!"

"You talk about President Kennedy?"

"Yes, I do. Yes, I do. I do speak of the president," Alphonsus assured him.

"Oh, yes. He was a good man."

There was a pause after the cabbie made his judgement, as he leaned forward slightly to peer through his windshield. The snow fell heavily as he manoeuvred down a sloping, winding hill toward the waterfront area, where the wharf lights and some ship lights glistened beyond the dark empty office buildings.

"Stop! Stop the car!" said Alphonsus, suddenly.

The taxi driver slowed the car and steered it to the side of the street, then stopped, pressing on the emergency lights.

"I have to keep the meter running," he said.

"That's all right. Worry not about the meter. I just want to show you something. You seem like an intelligent and sensitive man."

A light was switched on while Alphonsus removed a bulky leather wallet from his breast coat pocket and took out a folded white card, smudged and crumpled at one side because it didn't fit in the wallet properly.

Alphonsus opened the card carefully and read aloud while the car motor hummed and the meter ticked on.

"We are consoled to know that you share our sorrow, and that the love he gave is returned in good measure . . . . Blessed are they who mourn, for they shall be comforted. Blessed are they who hunger and thirst for justice, for they shall be fulfilled. Blessed are the peacemakers for they shall be called the children of God.' Matthew, fifth chapter, third verse. This is from Ethel. See? That's her signature. It's been almost ten years ago now," he said, thrusting it out and allowing the driver a quick look at it.

After Bobby Kennedy had been assassinated in 1968, Alphonsus had sent a card of sympathy to the Kennedy family and had received a thank you card from Ethel Kennedy, Bobby's widow.

The cab continued along the waterfront road, widened over recent years with bright light standards placed intermittently.

Champlain Street was one of the oldest streets in Quebec City, with houses built back in the 1800s.

Alphonsus still had his wallet in his hand so he removed a five-dollar bill from it as the car came to a stop. The meter read $4.25. The driver turned the handle. He looked at Alphonsus, who handed him the five. Alphonsus then pushed the car door open and, grunting, got out of the taxi.

"Thank you, sir," the cabbie said, his voice raised.

Alphonsus slammed the door shut and carefully placed himself on the sidewalk.

"Hey!" he yelled.

The taxi driver, who had already begun to drive away, stopped and backed his car to where Alphonsus stood. He leaned across the front seat and lowered the window.

"What is it?" he asked.

"Keep the change," said Alphonsus.

The taxi driver uttered a French profanity and skidded off, the window of the car still open.

The street was empty. Alphonsus stood on the sidewalk in the shallow wet snow, enjoying his solitude, the feeling of well-being.

He'd not worn his overshoes today so his socks were becoming damp as the wetness worked its way through the soles of his shoes. It felt good, his feet moist and cool. He could stand here for hours, just basking in the silence. But his bladder ached for release.

He looked up at the second-storey flat where he lived with his mother and his younger sister Katherine.

Katy for short, although she didn't like to be called Katy.
There was that dim light on in the living room. They
were watching the late movie again. Probably *"King Kong
Meets the Vampire,"* starring Umeshi Fujiyama, made in
Kyoto.

"Don't worry about the Japanese," had said Pat
Brennan earlier at Hogan's Tavern. "They came from
nowhere after the war, after Truman dropped the big A
on them."

"Harry Truman was the best god-damn president
the U.S. ever had!" had stated Benny Slater.

"Jack Kennedy would never have dropped a nuclear
weapon on the heads of the Japanese people," had said
Alphonsus. "He would at least have shown them what he
had. He would have exploded one on the top of a mountain or off the coast to show the Japanese what he had."

"Come on, Al," had said Tom Ellis. "Kennedy was
just a peacock who spent his time chasing after women."

"You're right, Tom," had agreed Benny Slater.
"That's what he was. A peacock."

At that point, Alphonsus had left. He had argued
with them for hours, and he was tired of it, fed up with
their inanities.

Now standing alone on the street in front of his flat,
he composed himself before he began to climb the stairway. He stuffed his wallet back into his suit pocket.

And where were his gloves? God-dammit, he'd left
them in the taxi. No, he'd left them at Hogan's. He wasn't
sure.

They had hidden his new leather gloves, that's it!
The bastards at Hogan's had hidden them, just like they
had hidden his overshoes last week, and his magazines,
and once even a fifty-dollar pair of shoes he had bought.

Then when he showed up again, they would give whatever they had hidden back to him, bellow their laughter, holding their sides, looking at each other for acknowledgement. The bastards! How they baited him!

On one occasion they had surreptitiously removed Pat Brennan's guitar from its case and filled the case with several old overshoes and Pat had then left the bar to sing for the old folks at St. Bridget's Home. About a half an hour later they'd gotten a phone call from Pat begging them to send the guitar up in a taxi, which they finally did. Gawd, how they had laughed that night! Alphonsus had laughed too, he had to admit. It was goddamn funny, when you thought about it. And it was all Bill Hogan's doing, you know; he was the mastermind behind all the mischief, and how innocent he could look.

"Who? Me?" he'd say. "Hey, I'm running a business here."

Alphonsus walked up the dark stairway, slowly but steadily. Rhythm was the important thing here. If the rhythm was irregular, they'd know he'd had too much to drink, and he didn't want Katy and his mother to think that.

When he got to the top of the stairs and grasped for the door knob, he found that the door was locked. He had no key, so he rapped on the door with his fist and stood waiting in the darkness. The door seemed to open by itself then, or was that the sound of his sister running back into the living room in her slippers?

Alphonsus let himself in, removed his spring-and-fall coat, and hung it in the hall closet—but not before knocking down a few cardboard boxes that were too big for the shelf over the coat rack. Actually, he tried to catch them before they hit the floor, but in reaching out

51

quickly, he knocked something else over, a broom or something—he couldn't tell.

"Everything okay, Al?" he heard his mother call.

He didn't answer but went to the living room doorway and stood there looking at the television set. His mother and sister were engrossed in the movie. Neither looked at him. He'd arrived in the middle of a love scene: Alan Ladd was making out with Virginia Mayo. Alphonsus let out a few fake coughs as both his mother and sister were smoking, the living room smelling somewhat like Hogan's tavern.

He ducked into the toilet. Sweet release. Then to the kitchen. Alphonsus looked in the fridge and the lower cupboards for a beer but could find none, so he decided to make himself a cup of coffee.

He put the kettle on the electric stove with just enough water in it for himself, and sat down at the kitchen table and sang, clapping his hands:

"I'm a rambler, I'm a gambler
I'm a long way from home
And if you don't like me
Then leave me alone."

Katy appeared at the kitchen door and told him to shut up, that they were trying to watch the movie.

Alphonsus sang again—a verse from the song, "Rosin the Bow," recorded by the Clancy Brothers.

"I hear that old tyrant approaching
That cruel remorseless old foe
And I lift up me glass in his honour
Have a drink with old Rosin the Bow."

The kettle was soon boiling on the stove so he got out a mug and the jar of instant coffee from the cupboard.

"Your kettle's boiling, Al!" he heard his mother shout from the living room.

"Up your arse!" he said quietly, even gently, making sure they'd never hear.

Just how would he break the news to them? How would they react? His father would have said, "Good, Alphonsus. I'm tickled that you finally decided. The Lord said, 'It's not good for man to live alone.'"

Alphonsus put two heaping spoons of sugar into his coffee, stirred it, and sipped it, humming from the song: "I'll Take You Home Again, Kathleen," putting in a few words here and there.

He had had a good voice as a kid, they'd all told him, singing in the St. Patrick's Day concert at the theatre. Right after Christmas they'd start practising with the good Sisters of Charity.

"Come in here!" he said loudly. "I'd like a few words with both of you."

There was no answer from the living room. Alphonsus got up and tiptoed into the hallway; the movie was still on.

"It's almost finished," said his mother, Margaret.

She had spoken loudly, not realizing that Alphonsus was in the hallway watching the cigarette smoke drift through the coloured patterns reflecting from the television set.

The good Sisters of Charity, thought Alphonsus, with their long black soutanes and the big white starched bibs and collars pinching against their reddened faces. At dismissal time in the afternoon, he remembered, they marched the girls out of school to the tune of "Anchors Away" or some other march left over from wartime, and he had stood there watching the girls flood down the stairway, with the large nun who played the piano at the foot of the stairs thumping at the keys without looking, which had amazed him.

At that time, Alphonsus would fetch Katy at the girls' school and walk home with her virtually across the city and down the steps to the Cove. They'd gone up and down those steps "thousands of times," flights of stairs which descended three hundred feet from the Plains of Abraham to Champlain Street.

On their way home from school, Alphonsus and Katy had had to pass "the Huts" every day. These ramshackle structures, which had been used during the Second World War to house German war prisoners, had been turned into public housing units after the war. The poorest of the city lived there.

Alphonsus dreaded passing by "the Huts" daily, but they'd had no other choice of route. It was the only way to get to the steps unless one wanted to risk death by sliding down the three-hundred-foot cliff. The safest way to handle this situation was to go through this rough area in a large group. There was some safety in numbers, but it was not always possible to improvise a group gathering for the gauntlet. The kids from Champlain Street usually ran through that section to avoid trouble. Stones would sail out from between the huts and lots of kids were hit. Once they made the steps, all were safe, because the gangs from the Huts would not venture down onto Champlain Street. Rumbles on the steps were infrequent, although to use the stairs at night time was considered risky. Then, in the early sixties, the Huts were totally removed and forever erased from the face of Battlefield Park.

Alphonsus returned to the kitchen, very quietly. He reached for the photo albums that his mother kept on the shelves of a little bookcase, and began to look through one of them. There were pictures of both his mother and father as youngsters. Her ancestors were the Slavins and some of them had farmed in an Irish community north of Quebec City. Some photos showed his mother squinting into the sun, in front of farm buildings and farm implements, along with cousins, many of whom he had met at weddings and funerals. There were also pictures of his uncles and aunts and cousins, with Cape Diamond as a background, one of the landmark names given to the high promontory which confronted the people who lived on Champlain Street. In the pictures taken during winter, ice pans could be seen in the distance, on the majestic St. Lawrence River.

A freeway now ran through the area next to the river. Only a thin strand of houses remained on the spot not far from where General Wolfe had scaled the cliffs with his army to emerge on the Plains of Abraham and do battle with the French General Montcalm in 1759.

"You want a cup of coffee, Ma?" said Katy, entering the kitchen.

"Did Mr. Ladd finally succeed in putting her to bed?" asked Alphonsus.

"You pick a hell of a time to start singing, at one o'clock in the morning. The neighbours must think we're nuts here."

"Where is Mother?"

"She's watching the late news."

"I wish to speak with both of you."

"Ma? Come in here!" said Katy, leaning into the hallway.

Margaret Kerwin soon shuffled into the kitchen, almost dragging one leg. She'd broken her hip the past winter, ten months ago now, and had been hospitalized for over three weeks as a result.

"God, my leg gets so stiff," she complained. "Al, put the albums back on the shelf, will you, if you're finished with them?"

She butted a cigarette out into a small ashtray on the kitchen table.

"Are you listening now?" warned Alphonsus.

"Yes, why?" said Margaret.

Both women looked at him.

"Sit down, for God's sake!" he said.

They both sat on chairs at the table.

"Cecile and I are getting married in April," he announced. "How does that grab you?"

"You're drunk!" said Katy.

"But you weren't with her tonight, were you?" asked Margaret.

"We're getting married at St. Dominic's Church," Alphonsus reiterated.

They looked at him incredulously. There was silence, save for Alphonsus sipping his coffee. Katy rose from her chair and put more water in the kettle, then placed two coffee mugs on the table.

"Where you gonna live?" she asked, still startled, her eyes widened.

"Uptown. I'm getting out of here," he said.

"I never realized you'd be that serious for her, Al," uttered Margaret. She leaned forward, resting her face in her hands then, her blue-veined wrists taut. She was a slender woman of sixty-four years of age.

"I'll believe it when I see it," Katy said.

"It's no concern of mine whether you believe me or not. The important thing is that I've told you."

"You're not gonna change, you know, just because you get married. You'll be the same person. She'll spend many a night waiting up for you, wherever the hell you're gonna live."

Margaret pleaded, "Katy, there's nothing to be gained by arguing at this time of the morning." Her voice was hushed.

"And what about Ma?" Katy continued. "You gonna leave her alone down here by herself? Who's gonna pay for the rent and the food?"

"Why? You planning on taking a one-way trip somewhere?" said Alphonsus, facetiously.

"Oh, don't worry about that. We'll make out all right," assured Margaret.

"Sure, you'll do all right. If Katy decided to move her ass and go back to work," he said, mockingly, to his mother.

"You know, Alphonsus," said Katy. "I feel sorry for Cecile. She's gonna marry a guy who loves his booze more than her. I feel sorry for you too, because you were born to make people miserable."

With that, she left the kitchen, the kettle whistling.

"Good night, K-K-K-Katy!" sneered Alphonsus.

Margaret took a crumpled handkerchief from the sleeve of her dress and sighed softly into it.

He hadn't proposed to Cecile as yet. He planned to do that soon. They would both be working and could share the cost of keeping house.

"And why are you sniffling, Mother?"

"Because you and Katherine are forever at each other's throats."

"Well, she is a basket case."

Up until the death of her father, Katy had always

worked, but shortly after the funeral she had left her job with the company she'd been with for close to a dozen years and had begun to collect unemployment insurance. This ran out after a year and her income was then reduced to whatever she picked up doing temporary work for "Office Overload" and brief periods of employment at a number of places. Lately, she'd become a sort of a recluse and ventured out little except for the summertime when she lay on the back veranda facing the river and suntanned herself.

Certainly, Alphonsus could not figure out what had happened to her. His jibes and taunts did not seem to prod her sense of pride sufficiently. Surely he was doing more than his share. Did he not give more than half of his salary to his mother every payday? If he got married, he would not be able to continue these contributions, and keep his own apartment at the same time.

* * *

The first, faint light of morning began to show in his window that faced the open expanse of water. Alphonsus must have fallen asleep as he listened to the Irish music he had put on his stereo. The needle on the record player was scratching rhythmically, so he got up from his bed and shut the system off. His looked at his small alarm clock-radio. It showed 6:00 a.m. It would be full daylight in a few hours. He felt too lazy to get undressed, and sensed that he would not sleep any more. It had to be his drinking. He had been drinking too much lately. Yesterday he'd had no supper, just beer for six hours straight. How much had he drunk anyway? He couldn't remember. He felt sober now. He sat up on the side of the bed and put his right thumb on his left wrist to feel his pulse.

He decided he would get undressed and get under the covers. He removed his tie, shirt, and trousers and looked at himself in the dresser mirror. He was putting on weight again, especially around the stomach and kidneys. He snapped off the light of the lamp beside his bed and stretched out beneath the blankets.

The sun was blazing into his window when the alarm went off. He had managed to sleep a little more, but he had a headache now, as usual, and lay in his bed, his eyes sticky, yearning to sleep longer. He pulled himself up and squinted through the window at the river, where a tanker was at anchor out in the middle near the oil storage complex.

When he stepped out of his doorway on another November morning, the half-dozen people gathered waiting for the bus were all shivering.

He disliked the grip of winter, when his glasses fogged, and his nose ran, and his ears froze. The only saving grace was the knowledge that a warm chair awaited him at Hogan's any cold evening after he could leave the hell-hole which was his office. He sat in that thin glass cubicle surrounded by chattering people around the front desk, facing the selfish moon-faces of the bellhops across the lobby, and putting up with the bronzed presence of Boileau, the hotel manager.

It was twenty years now since he'd graduated from high school and started work for the local English newspaper. He had wanted to get into the writing and reporting end of it, but there never seemed to be an opening, so he got fed up with doing clerical work and joined the staff of the hotel as a room clerk, having vague and romantic aspirations of rising in the business and being the manager of some posh mecca in Montreal, or even Switzerland.

At the hotel, after working the day shift for a few years, he was "promoted" to the position of night Office Manager, and had accepted it only to grow to detest it later because of the long hours of boredom. The job had consisted mainly of registering late-comers and helping the house detective ease drunks out of the lobby. Between 2:00 a.m. and 6:00 a.m., very little happened and he usually sat behind the counter, reading or dozing off, or walking up and down to avoid falling asleep. The odd straggler or disoriented guest would wander up to the desk and ask some inane question, such as: "Is there a swimming pool in this hotel?" There wasn't. Alphonsus put up with this for six years. His dad had told him to be patient, that one rose slowly in the hotel business.

Finally, the position of Front Office Manager, a daytime job, was thrown open when the then manager was transferred to Montreal. Alphonsus was given the vacated post and a considerable raise in salary, which he was happy to accept because of his increasing practice of consuming ample quantities of alcoholic beverages and squandering money on tips to late-working waitresses and then on the taxi rides home.

It was at Hogan's tavern where Alphonsus began to renew old acquaintances, from high school mainly. They would meet there almost daily during the week and talk, argue, laugh, and torment each other until closing time around midnight. There was no topic that they were not willing to discuss. Often they were quite loud and had to be warned by Bill Hogan, the proprietor of the tavern, to tone it down. He was afraid that their unquenchable thirst for argument would keep other customers away, including

French-speaking clients who might find the bar handy. He would sometimes find it necessary to order one of the debaters out if that person became too obnoxious, or if the subject matter under discussion was volatile. Months could go by before the expelled person would make a re-appearance, swallowing his pride, but inevitably he would return.

No doubt, Bill Hogan would have found his evenings rather dull if some of the group did not show up. For when he had a free moment, which wasn't often, he would pull up a chair and join the conversation or argument, or tell a joke, or listen to the latest gossip.

The Chateau Frontenac Hotel, where Alphonsus toiled, was quiet this time of year, the in-between season, after the summer tourist period was long over, and before the Christmas Holidays and the Winter Carnival festivities began.

Both room clerks looked at Alphonsus as he entered the front office area, interrupting the conversation they were sharing. He took a quick look at the key rack which told him that the hotel was about half occupied.

"Good morning, Mr. Kerwin," said Mary Power, the young woman who typed his letters and handled incoming mail.

"Morning, Mary," answered Alphonsus.

The other people in the office did not look at him; at least, he did not think they did. He knew he was not that popular in the front office, due to his unwillingness to exchange idle banter.

He went into his glass-surrounded cubicle from where he kept an eye on the whole front office operation, and switched his desk lamp on. He sat down and began reading the mail that Mary Power had left on his desk.

At 10:00 a.m., Alphonsus walked quickly down to

the hotel's Terrace Cocktail Lounge, a room with floor-to-ceiling windows that faced the boardwalk overlooking the St. Lawrence River two hundred feet below.

What he needed was a shot of something. His headache was almost gone, and he felt that a belt would put him back on the right track.

"Hey, Herve," he said softly to the bartender. "Slip me a Chivas."

"No Chivas left. I got the other."

"Okay."

The bartender fixed the drink for Alphonsus and tucked it into a small niche behind the bar. Alphonsus was not to drink on the premises. That was the unwritten rule. But he had an arrangement with Herve Cantin where the bartender placed a drink at the disposal of Alphonsus, unobserved.

"Quiet, Herve?"

"Sure is. I hate this time of year."

"Well, just take it easy. It'll pick up."

"I hate taking it easy."

"How's the wife?"

"Frigid as a polar bear."

"Maybe you're just not a good lover," teased Alphonsus.

"You speaking from experience, choirboy?"

"Just give me a little time with your wife and I'll program her for you."

"You couldn't program an outhouse."

"When you gonna get some Chivas Regal?"

"Never."

"Get some Chivas or I'll take my business elsewhere."

"Please do."

"Who drinks it all, anyway?"

"You do."

"What do you mean? I haven't been down here since last week."

"Everybody knows you drink here. By the way, your tab is up to close to fifty bucks."

"Pay you next week."

"You'd better. It's coming out of my pocket, don't forget. Now, fuck off, Al. I got customers."

Alphonsus downed the remainder of the Scotch, put the glass back behind the bar. He observed a group of three businessmen-types take a table beside one of the large windows, then turned and went back up to his office.

*   *   *

Cecile Martin pulled herself up after having lain in the bathtub, allowing the warm water to soothe her tiredness. She dried her slender body with a large, fluffy towel and then looked at herself in the steam-covered mirror over the wash basin and shelf. She lifted her arms up over her head and watched her breasts and the flesh of her rib area as it thinned out to reveal the underlying rows of chest bones.

She could then hear the telephone ringing and the muffled voice of her mother answering it.

"Cil? Telephone!" her mother called near the bathroom door. "Will you answer it?"

"Yes, yes. I'm coming." Cecile answered.

She knew it was Alphonsus. He usually called her about this time. She wondered if he was at the bar again. She threw on her bathrobe and went out to the telephone in the hallway of the apartment. She sensed the ears of her mother listening even though the latter pretended to be reading a newspaper.

"Allo, Al?" She spoke in French to him as usual.

"Hi, Cecile. How's it going?"

"Everything's fine. Where are you?"

"I'm at a restaurant having a bite to eat."

"I can hear loud voices. It sounds like a bar or a tavern."

"And how were the little monsters today?" Alphonsus didn't want to dwell on his whereabouts.

"You mean at school? Oh, terrible! I don't know if it's the cold weather, but some of them are pretty excited. I just took a long bath there, and was trying to relax."

She'd first met Alphonsus four months before on a beautiful July evening during a band concert at La Citadelle de Québec, the famous old fortification that was perched high above the St. Lawrence River. The concert had been performed by the Van Doos Regiment Band, a group of surprisingly well trained military musicians who played everything from Bach to Glenn Miller music. She had gone there with a girlfriend.

When she first saw Alphonsus she took him to be an American tourist since he spoke English, a little loudly, with his companion, Pat Brennan. Her friend, Louise Filion, had turned around a few times to caution them or give them a cold stare. But they had kept up their banter, laughing at stories they were telling each other.

Cecile had wondered what he would look like and she turned around and allowed her eyes to wander over the crowd of hundreds of people lounging on the long, grassy slope which eased down to the bandstand. She was attracted to that clear lyrical voice and wanted to have a look at the face that went with the voice. When their eyes met, he was already staring right at her face.

Alphonsus and his friend then began to tease them quietly.

"Come to my little hacienda in New Mexico, so peaceful and quiet in the high Sierra Mountains," pleaded Alphonsus, doing his imitation of Danny Kaye. "There we can kiss and caress and forget about the Parti Québécois."

A rash of chuckling would follow these kinds of remarks. Cecile's friend Louise suggested that the two of them move to an area closer to the band, but Cecile had discouraged her. An hour or so later the four of them were walking along Dufferin Terrace, above the river, rubbing shoulders and speaking French.

She was impressed with Alphonsus from the beginning. He expressed himself extremely well in French, though he did make grammatical errors that she sometimes corrected. He had picked up the second language "on the street" since he had attended English high school. Her English was not nearly as proficient as his French, even if she struggled hard to improve it. Alphonsus later gave her English books to read and while watching English television and movies, he was very helpful in making her understand. But mostly they conversed in French.

"You busy tonight?" asked Alphonsus.

"Well, I'm pretty tired. It's already quite late. Why? What have you got in mind?"

"Oh, I don't know. I'd like to see you, that's all."

"Have you been drinking?"

"No, of course not. I hardly ever drink during the week. You know that."

"Oh? Do I?"

She had discovered that about Al. He enjoyed a drink. Too much, she thought. She wondered if she should get too involved with him because of this factor.

She drove her small Japanese car through the rather bitter coolness of the old city. It was late but Alphonsus had sounded excited about something and wanted to see her. She wondered what was on his mind, sensing it was probably about their future together. What would she say if he proposed to her? They had already spoken about getting together, rather off-handedly, on a few occasions but he hadn't really made a direct proposition. She tried to imagine what it would be like living with him. He had always acted the gentleman while in her company. He was polite and considerate, and she almost always enjoyed being with him.

But did she love him enough to marry him? She certainly loved his sense of humour, the way he spoke French, his neat manner of dress. Yet he seemed to be reluctant to get involved with her family. He hit it off well with her father, but did not relate very well with her mother. Actually, she herself had difficulty getting along with her mother.

Her mother had always hoped that some prosperous type would have sought Cecile's hand in marriage, and not the glorified room clerk who spoke French with an odd accent. So she had resented Alphonsus somewhat, though she never said so to Cecile.

She certainly would have preferred it if Cecile had stuck with Jean-Charles, the salesman Cecile had gone with for years. But, of course, he'd been so laggard, always putting things off. Jean-Charles had regretted his procrastinating behaviour since Cecile had started going with "L'Anglais" and made frequent phone calls to Cecile, often insistent and over-apologetic in tone.

Cecile parked her Toyota on Boulevard Grand-Allée and went into the Buffet des Employés Civils, where she and Alphonsus had eaten a few times before. It was a cozy little restaurant with a suitably spaced table arrangement where people could have a quiet conversation. Soft music permeated the pastel-painted atmosphere of the room.

"You got here fast," said Alphonsus, standing up as she approached. His eyes half-mockingly looked her up and down. "You look beautiful, as usual."

He took her coat, went to a wall rack, and carefully placed it on a hanger.

"Thank you," she said then, seating herself.

"Are you hungry?" he asked.

"Not really. I've had supper. But I see you've helped yourself to a drink."

"Would you like to try what I'm drinking?" asked Alphonsus.

"And what is it?"

"Scotch on the rocks. Chivas Regal. Only the best for the Irish."

"No, thank you. That's terrible stuff."

Alphonsus signalled the waitress and Cecile ordered a soft drink.

"You told me you don't drink during the week, "she said.

"I don't normally, but since this is a special occasion, I thought I'd have a drink."

Cecile felt a surge of expectation.

"What's the special occasion?"

She looked into his eyes.

"Well, I thought we should get serious and talk about . . . us," said Alphonsus, shrugging his shoulders. He looked at his glass as he spoke and appeared somewhat self-conscious.

"Do you have something specific to discuss?" she said.

"Yes. Yes, I guess I have."

"What is it?"

"Well . . . we should get married."

"That's not a question," she said quickly, and laughed.

The waitress arrived with Cecile's beverage and an awkward silence ensued for a moment. The restaurant was sparsely filled but Alphonsus and Cecile felt obliged to speak softly, since a group of girls sat near them.

"I thought we could announce our engagement at Christmas and get married in the spring," offered Alphonsus.

Cecile's eyes were suddenly misty. She retrieved a kleenex from a small packet in her handbag and wiped her nose. Alphonsus realized he was seeing another side of her now. He'd never seen her close to tears.

"It's so . . . it's so extraordinary. It's so sudden," she murmured. "We hardly know each other. We're so different."

"Different? What do you mean, different? I'm a man and you're a woman. That's different. But we're both Catholics. We've never been married before. I don't see any major problem."

"But I hardly know you, Al," she repeated. "We don't really do things together, except go out to places and eat and drink on weekends."

"What's there to know? I've known you for over four months now. I'm not asking you to marry me tomorrow. We'll get to know each other better over the next many months."

She reached across the table and grasped his hands. An elderly couple came in and sat at the table closest to them. The woman looked at them, passively, and Alphonsus pulled his hands away from Cecile's. They sat, looking at their drinks for a moment.

"I think," Cecile said, leaning forward, "it's something we should think about for awhile."

Alphonsus didn't respond. Had she turned him down? Was she actually declining the offer? He had pictured her being overwhelmed at his proposal, embarrassing him with her acceptance. There were a few more moments of silence between them, now uncomfortable.

Alphonsus suddenly rose, placed a ten-dollar bill on the table, walked over and reached for his coat on the wall, and left her.

"Al!" she called after him.

He continued to walk, down the street from the restaurant. He could have sworn he heard her calling after him, but he wasn't sure. He didn't bother to turn around but trudged swiftly away, down Grande-Allée and through the Parliament Buildings area where the National Assembly building stood, not heeding the elements, his coat unbuttoned, his pride, the victim of a sagacious assault, deeply offended.

Later, Cecile sat in her car outside the high-rise where she lived with her parents. What had come over Alphonsus? What had she said to make him react that way? His behaviour had angered her at first: leaving her there in a restaurant with half a dozen people staring at her.

She wondered about Alphonsus now. Was that how he would treat her if they started to live and sleep together, by simply walking away from a situation that required an element of tenderness or patience or understanding?

One day she had asked him about his father and what he had been like, and Al had told her of the circumstances surrounding his father's death. After talking about it, he had lost momentary control then, too— becoming inflamed and cursing the government for keeping his father in financial turpitude. Tears had welled in his eyes and when she had put her arm around him, he had pulled away. Even if he had later apologized she felt there was a side of him that she could never reach, never succeed in coddling.

Yet some of the most pleasant evenings she'd spent in her life had been in the last few months when Al would bring her to parties at the homes of some of his friends. Being an outsider, she did not get all the jokes, or nuances, but nonetheless she'd been a thoroughly contented spectator, feeling accepted. Several of the wives of Al's friends were Québécoises, whom she attached herself to very easily.

She felt now that she had severely injured Al's pride. No doubt he had expected her to accede to his proposal—a once-in-a-lifetime question that a man saves for the right place and time. But she had, in a sense, turned him down by refusing to answer affirmatively.

As a lover, Alphonsus was no Don Juan. He did not dispense affection openly but rather like a benevolent uncle secretly giving money to a favourite niece. They had not shared a deluge of passion together since she had known him. On one occasion early in their relationship, while they were watching a late movie on television, she had kissed Al many times and had then opened her mouth and had run her tongue over his lips. He drew back suddenly and laughed, taken by surprise. It was as if he'd not realized that such a thing could naturally happen when two people were in the midst of a loving kiss.

* * *

"Alphonsus, you bastard! Come and sit down! Is it cold out, Al? Are we gonna have an early winter?"

Benny Slater greeted Alphonsus at Hogan's Tavern, while he lit another cigarette, a seemingly unending habit of his which saw him obfuscate the area around the table with clouds of smoke. His greeting to Alphonsus went unanswered.

Tom Ellis, seated with Benny Slater, laughed at the coarse reception. Alphonsus removed his topcoat, hung it, and pulled up a chair to sit with them at the table.

"Big one, Bill," called Alphonsus.

Bill Hogan smiled as he placed a tall bottle of beer before Alphonsus.

"You look as if you just got fired."

"Not a chance, Bill. I feel just fine," Alphonsus lied.

"Can't be too many people up at the hotel these days?"

"Oh, Gawd, no," said Alphonsus, pouring his beer into a draft glass. "One of the little jerks at the desk didn't show up so I had to go up and hold the fort."

He was not going to talk about what had happened between him and Cecile, certainly. He did not want to be the focus of attention on this evening. He just wanted to have some beer and forget about things for a while.

71

"So, Benny," said Alphonsus. "You still struggling with the cadres in the Income Tax Department?'

"Yep. But I work for the federal government, not the provincial. Don't forget that!" said Benny Slater.

"You must be the only English-speaking guy up there."

"Just about," said Slater, "but there's still a few of us. They're bloody glad to have us."

"I suppose there isn't much chance of you getting a managerial position up there, is there?"

" I don't know, Alphonsus. Maybe I don't want to be a department head."

"Maybe if you had a French surname, you'd have a better chance. I mean, Slater is a bit too anglophone, isn't it?" suggested Alphonsus.

"There goes Kerwin! The old prejudice showing up again. You're a bigot, Alphonsus!" chastised Ellis. He accentuated the name Alphonsus.

"I'm no more bigoted than the next guy. I call it as I see it. I call a spade a spade."

"You're frustrated, Al," continued Ellis. "You hate speaking French even though you're in a French city and a French province. You hate having to read French and having to hear French spoken every day. Why don't you get out of the province like the rest of the quitters who left?"

"People who have left this province are still Canadians."

"Canadians? They're quitters, that's what they are!"

There was an odd period of quiet. The tavern was almost empty. Alphonsus reached into his breast coat pocket for his wallet. He extracted a small newspaper clipping from one of the slits.

"Here, Mr. Ellis," Alphonsus said. "I want you to read this. Read it aloud so you'll be able to hear it and understand it. It concerns the plans of the government to have English-speaking professionals submit to language proficiency tests in French."

He reached across the table with the clipping and tried to get Ellis to take it.

"Here he comes with his god-damn clippings again!" blurted Ellis. He refused to accept it from Alphonsus, waving an arm toward him.

"Now you're acting like an ignoramus," said Alphonsus.

"Kerwin, you call me an ignoramus once more and I'll punch your face in!" Ellis exploded.

He rose from his chair, but Bill Hogan and Benny Slater got in his way and dissuaded him from advancing toward Alphonsus, who was still seated.

"All right, let's calm down now, or we'll have to call it a night," warned Bill Hogan, leaning on the table and staring at Ellis.

"Aren't we just like the Irish, fighting among ourselves!" said Benny Slater.

Ellis sat down again and took a swig of his beer.

"I apologize, Thomas. I get pretty riled up over this stuff," said Alphonsus.

Benny attempted to cajole Ellis. "All right, Tom. He apologizes. So let's simmer down now."

Bill Hogan went back to behind the bar.

"Lookit, Tom," Alphonsus was more conciliatory in his tone, "if you ask an English-speaking nurse some questions in French, questions that don't apply to medicine, you'll be able to tell by her answers how good she is in French. But that's got nothing to do with her field of nursing. She might be another Florence Nightingale, but the government doesn't care. They like these tests because they get the kind of information they like. Her value as a nurse is decided by a French test."

"Isn't that what all exams are about?" queried Ellis. "I mean, didn't we write final exams in high school to see what we knew?"

"That's right," agreed Alphonsus, "but, you see, the tests show how much French she knows, not how good a nurse she is. The score of eighty-two means more competence than a score of sixty-two. It's very simple for the government. The tests give us what the government calls objectivity and clarity and precision. There's nothing that we seem to be able to do about this. No wonder people get frustrated and nervous and they start moving out of the province."

Ellis was not impressed.

"If the English," he argued, "stuck to their guns and worked together, and started throwing a few rocks around, the government wouldn't be so eager to give tests to the English. There is little unity among the English-speaking people in Quebec. You know, the English are very class-conscious. They like to be top dog. A lot of them left Quebec because they could see they weren't gonna be top dog any more. It's a lot easier for them to just pack up and leave, rather than stay and fight."

"Okay, Tom," Alphonsus persisted. "Now, let's suppose that the government wins the next referendum and the Office de la Langue Francaise decides to give all anglophones who deal with the public a language test. Wouldn't that include you? You deal with the public, don't you?"

"I could never see the government doing that," said Ellis.

"Yeah, of course they could do it," put in Benny Slater. "People like teachers, government clerks who're English, bank clerks, people who work in department stores, gas station attendants, funeral directors, tourist people, taxi drivers. Why not? The government could do it!"

"The question is," said Alphonsus, pointing across the table to Tom Ellis, "could you, Tom Ellis, pass a written French test in grammar and composition, subject to the passing mark they want?"

"Sure I could."

"Oh, yeah? I'm not so sure. You never went to French school. You learned your French on the street just like I did," said Alphonsus. "So suppose the pass mark was seventy-two or something like that. The question is, Tom, would you pass? From what I heard, you didn't exactly set any records in high school."

Alphonsus did not see Tom Ellis swing his fist quickly across the table. But he felt a thunderous blow on his cheek and left eye, and suddenly blinded, he sensed himself falling into space, small white flashes of light, like hundreds of tumbling and rising stars, swirling past his field of vision.

When he came to, he was lying on the floor and glimpsed a whirl of activity about him with lots of yelling and curses, falling chairs, and nudged tables. Benny Slater and Bill Hogan were evidently attempting to subdue Tom Ellis, who was intent upon getting to Alphonsus to rain more blows upon him.

Still dizzy and shaking his head to clear it, Alphonsus brought his hand up to his face. He could feel the area below his left eye already swelling. He looked at his fingers then but could see no blood.

Bill Hogan and Benny Slater soon managed to sit Ellis down on a chair against the wall away from Alphonsus. Benny held onto Ellis while Bill came over to Alphonsus and bent down to minister to him.

"Are you all right, Alphonsus?"

"Yes, Bill. I'm fine."

"Well, then . . . can you get up?"

He helped Alphonsus to his feet, then picked up a chair and straightened out the table.

Alphonsus sat down again, hand on his cheek, patting the unrelenting swell, feeling the eye close.

Bill Hogan soon had his broom out, sweeping up pieces of bottle and glass that had splintered during the one-sided and brief encounter. He then went to Tom Ellis and spoke quietly to him. Ellis stood, went for his coat, walked briskly to the door, and disappeared.

"I don't like to say it, Alphonsus, but you had it coming," said Bill Hogan, sitting in Tom Ellis's vacant chair.

"I have to agree, Alphonsus. You know what he's like," agreed Benny Slater.

"You have a way of making a guy feel like two cents," went on Bill Hogan. "I'll give you credit for winning some arguments, but your mouth works against you."

"The fucker!" murmured Alphonsus, "He's gonna pay for it this time." He spoke softly, head down, embarrassed, defeated, fingering his cheek. He could hardly see out of his left eye now, the swelling having almost completely closed it. Bill Hogan got up, went to his refrigerator and wrapped some ice cubes in a dish-towel, and gave it to Alphonsus who pressed it against his face.

"Forget it, Alphonsus," counselled Bill. "Just take it as a lesson learned. You called him an ignoramus and you insulted his intelligence, so I don't see how you're gonna make him pay."

"Best thing to do is to forget about it, Al," said Benny.

"I'll never forget it for the rest of my life. Would you? He's the same when you play touch football with him. Every chance he gets he tries to take your fucking head off!"

"Yeah, I always try to get him on my team," said Benny.

"You've got to admit it, Alphonsus. He's got a great overhand right," smiled Bill Hogan. "And if you keep the ice on it, the swelling will go down. Then it'll turn technicolour."

"Black, cadmium red, purple, and azure blue, with a little yellow on the outside," added Benny Slater.

Levity was entering into the incident now.

"See, Alphonsus," explained Bill Hogan, "the cells in your face are a disaster area right now, so your brain is responding by ordering emergency help from your white blood cells. Millions of cells around your eye have been totally obliterated but, fear not, help is on the way!"

"How am I supposed to explain this up at the hotel tomorrow?" moaned Alphonsus.

When Alphonsus left the tavern an hour or so later, the streets, shaded in a heavy November darkness, hid his swollen features. He'd already decided that he would call in sick the next day. There was no way that he could go to work with one of his eyes puffed up as it was. They would begin to talk about him when they noticed it.

He walked up to the taxi stand, went to the first car in the line-up, got in, and asked the driver to take him to

"La Grande Hermine," a bar at one of the hotels on Grande Allée Boulevard.

The bar was quiet as he sat in his customary stool, sipping a double Chivas Regal and mulling over the events of a rather crowded evening. The piano player soon showed up and people from a convention at the hotel, with identification badges on their lapels, began sauntering in. Soon a sing-song began. This perked Alphonsus up somewhat, but he stayed glued to his stool and consumed several more drinks.

When he emerged from the bar, it was well into the early hours, and he was well into drunkenness. After walking a piece, he hailed a taxi and slipped in beside the driver in the front seat. He was thankful for the cozy comfort of the car and began to sing for the benefit of the driver. He sang several verses of several songs, including "Bold O'Donohue" and "The Rising of the Moon."

The driver had to remind Alphonsus that they had reached his destination on Champlain Street. When Alphonsus opened his wallet to pay the driver, he was short at least two dollars.

"Sir! I happen to be lacking the funds to pay you your full amount. Would you accept the honourable proposition that I repay you on another occasion?" Alphonsus said.

"I'm sorry. I would like to be paid now," the driver replied, not amused.

"Very well, sir. Would you wait here? I shall return forthwith."

Alphonsus found the door handle, exited, and precariously set out to scale his pitch black stairway to acquire additional funds.

"Katy! Mother! Katy!" he shouted before he had

reached the second-floor landing. "Pass me a few bucks! The taxi guy's waiting!"

The door of the flat was locked, as usual.

"Jesus Christ! Open the door! Can't you see, the guy's waiting! Just pass me a few bucks!" yelled Alphonsus.

He hit the door with his fist. The crack under it lit up and he could hear movement from inside. The door opened.

"What is it, Alphonsus? Why in God's name are you making such a racket?" His mother stood in the doorway, looking down at him, shock registering in her face. "My god, Alphonsus, what's happened to you?"

Katy peeked out from her room down the hall.

"Good Jesus! He was in a fight or something!" she blurted.

"All I need is two god-damn dollars! I'll pay you back tomorrow," said Alphonsus, catching his breath.

"Here, Ma. Give it to him," said Katy.

Margaret Kerwin took the money from her daughter and passed it to Alphonsus, who immediately turned and began to fall down the stairway. Somehow he managed to maintain his balance and banged down the remaining steps. The outside door squealed and rapped several times before he came up again for the last time.

"You must be happy now that you've awakened the whole god-damn neighbourhood," said Katy in greeting.

"Aw, go to bed, you silly ass!" uttered Alphonsus, hanging his coat in the closet.

"Quiet, both of you!" cautioned Margaret.

But Katy went on: "You're the guy who's supposed to be getting married in a few months. You think your wife will be happy seeing you staggering in at two o'clock in the morning, cursing on the stairs? She'll never get used to that!"

"You shut your god-damn mouth or, so help me, I'll slap you one!"

He approached Katy, who stood at her bedroom doorway.

"Just you lay a hand on me and see what'll happen!" she warned him.

Margaret struggled to position herself between them, but she was too late. Alphonsus swung his hand sharply and struck his sister flush on the side of her face. After his impulsive act, he stood before his sister, stunned at his own unexpected willfulness.

Katy bent down, her hands covering her face. Then she looked up at him.

"You dirty bastard! You dirty bastard!"

"Stop it! Stop it, in the name of God!" pleaded Margaret.

Alphonsus went to his bedroom door, fumbled for and found his key, and escaped into his room. He sat in the lone chair in his bedroom, reeling at the tumultuous events of the day. A good stiff belt of Scotch would do right now. He could hear his sister yelling at him through the door about how she was about to call the police, her mother trying to placate her. The furor quietened down then, which enabled Alphonsus to tiptoe down the hall-way to the bathroom to relieve himself, his mother and sister talking in hushed tones in the kitchen. He returned to his room and put on an Irish record of soft Gaelic harp music.

His guilt consumed him. He lay on the bed, not too drunk to realize that his behaviour had mostly been the result of scape-goating. He got up and looked at himself in his dresser mirror. Puffy, reddened left eye, swollen cheek. He looked like a bum.

He removed all of his clothes and stood, naked, before the mirror again. Something within him was coming undone. His demeanour seemed no longer rational or civilized. He climbed under his bedcovers and soon fell into a harried sleep.

Later that morning, Remembrance Day, Alphonsus showered and shaved and called the hotel to say that he would not be in. Wearing sunglasses, he took the bus uptown and ducked into a restaurant on Côte de la Fabrique for some breakfast. He sat in the restaurant booth and read the morning newspaper, then walked up to the Cross of Sacrifice, the federal Memorial to the war dead, where Remembrance Day ceremonies were to be held. From several blocks away, he could see that hundreds of people had gathered for the annual event. Columns of servicemen and women were lined up about the monument—a simple, huge stone cross, some twenty-five feet in height. The steps leading to the cross were already adorned with wreaths, supported by delicate stands.

Alphonsus, with many others, stood on top of one of the three-foot-high concrete walls that surrounded the National Assembly building just across the street from the ongoing ceremony, to get a better view of the proceedings. An aura of subdued and solemn activity permeated the scene. Beret-topped old men, with saddened, serious faces, began walking in slow march up to the cross to lay more wreaths.

The music began, the low, haunting brass of the Van Doos band, in colourful garb, playing mournful pieces that gave the occasion yet more dignified meaning.

81

Then all stood still as a lone trumpeter stepped up to the monument and began playing the "Last Post." Downward bare heads bent, thin-haired veterans in the twilight of their years. An unrelenting curse was war, thought Alphonsus—contrived hate, unforgetting pain, where love of country had meant death to many. The Canadian war dead were all martyrs and saints, their bones scattered in some pasture in faraway lands, wild flowers growing over their graves, often arranged in symmetrical rows as they had marched.

Alphonsus found himself still standing on the wall long after the veterans had marched away and the crowd had dissipated. Two elderly women stopped on the sidewalk to look up at him, one of them snickering. He got down from the wall and crossed the street to edge close to the multi-coloured floral wreaths spread out at the foot of the cross. One read: "In memory of John and Stephen, who fell at Dieppe."

He took the city bus out to St. Patrick's Cemetery. It was situated a few miles west of the city, high up above the river. It was a beautiful place to be buried, thought Alphonsus, looking across at the panoramic view of the broad St. Lawrence and the distant blue mountains. He wondered if he would have an appreciation of this if he were interred here. Bright sunlight fell on leafless trees. The dirty grey of granite starkly blended with freshly placed red flowers on the graves.

Alphonsus stood before the small monument dedicated to his father, James Kerwin. He bowed his head and clasped his hands together. He said the Our Father and some Hail Marys and then tried to revive some memories.

Kerwin, James Patrick, 1918 to 1975, sitting by the window, sucking on his cigarette, with his Chronicle-

Telegraph spread out, reading the obituary column first. Leaving home late evenings to climb up the stairs to the Parliament Buildings where his job waited—night watchman—his brown sugar sandwiches and tea thermos packed into his black lunch pail. Arriving home from his nightshift just before Alphonsus and Katy left for school. Sitting on the rocking chair, his head nodding with sleepiness, his wife prodding him, "Go on to bed, Jim. Go ahead, now."

His father had been a quiet man. When he had offered advice to Alphonsus, which was seldom, it was brief and pithy. Alphonsus could not remember ever having been scolded by his father, although his mother was prone to raising her voice and threatening to slap him.

Alphonsus left the gravesite and walked down to the edge of the cemetery property facing the river and stood in the sunlight, the soft wind blowing dead leaves about his feet, watching a long freighter go up the river.

Searching for Mary Ann

ALPHONSUS TAPPED DOWN the long stairway, dozens of flights made of hardwood with rails on both sides, the only descending steps he knew of that tired him out.

In the old days, Paddy Fargo would be hanging around the foot of the stairway to Champlain Street, waiting for some kid to pick on. Alphonsus could still picture him leaning against the railing with a cigarette hanging from the corner of his mouth. Paddy must have started smoking at the age of seven.

"Hey, skinny!" Fargo would yell at Eleanor O'Malley as she came down the stairs. "Hey, skinny bones! Here comes E flat!"

All because Eleanor O'Malley was quite tall and very thin. Eleanor had a younger brother, Michael, who was even thinner and who told Fargo at school that he was fed up with Fargo's insults and wanted Fargo to wait for him after school. They were gonna have a punch-up, if only Fargo had the guts to wait for him.

"I'm gonna punch him out!" Michael told Alphonsus at the time, bravely, his voice shaking.

But before school was over that day, Michael had changed his mind. Fargo waited for Michael outside the school, in the yard.

Finally, Michael came out, with one of the teachers. Michael had told the teacher that Fargo was waiting outside the school to beat him up. So the teacher took Fargo into Brother Simon's office, and Fargo was kept there for at least an hour, twiddling his thumbs.

Fargo was furious about what had happened but he could do little about it. Nellie O'Malley, the mother of Michael and Eleanor, used to wait for her kids at the bottom of the stairs from then on. Nellie was tall and thin, too, but knarly as a barbed-wire fence, so Fargo would not have dared confront her.

* * *

"Who's that?" Alphonsus heard his mother's voice calling from the kitchen.

He did not answer immediately but hung his coat in the hall closet.

"It's your beloved son in whom you are not well pleased," said Alphonsus, entering the kitchen. "Where's Katy?"

"Talking to Mrs. Tremblay next door."

"Oh? Since when did she decide to venture outside the walls of the hermitage?"

"You haven't been home this early in months," suggested Margaret. She was sewing a large piece of brightly patterned material.

"Things are slow at the hotel."

"You gonna pick up those shoes of yours? They're on the porch there, full of mud."

"My shoes? What shoes?"

"You know. Those crazy shoes on the porch."

"Oh, yes. My football cleats."

"Whatever you call them. You'd better clean them up before they freeze."

"Any phone calls for me?"

"Al, there hasn't been a phone call for you here since God knows when. People know you don't live here any more. Oh, you sleep here, but that's about all."

"Any mail?"

"Just your *Time* magazine there."

She nodded her head toward the bookcase. Alphonsus picked up the magazine and began skimming through it.

"What date have you chosen to get married?" Margaret said, looking at him.

"Oh, we don't know yet. We're not sure. Sometime in April or May," he lied.

"Al, do you mind if I say a few things?"

"Mother, you know that sermons have very little effect on me."

"This is not a sermon. Just a little advice. You know, your father used to drink quite a lot just before we got married. But I told him . . ."

"I'm sure you did, Mother."

"I told him that if he didn't stop, I'd leave him."

"I don't remember Dad being drunk very often."

"Well, at first he didn't drink during the week but he used to make up for it on weekends. He used to hang around with that drunk Willie Carlisle, and he came home so drunk one night that he fell off the bed and I picked him up off the floor and he just threw himself onto the floor again. Another time he passed out in the bathroom and we had to break the door down. The neighbours came in to help me. But he just lay there on the floor and wouldn't let anyone touch him. He just lay there kicking at anyone who came near him. He was on the floor for hours."

Alphonsus had heard this story before.

"But things were very tough then," she continued, "just before the war, and I guess I don't blame him for getting drunk. There was no work to be found. Your father used to get odd jobs with the government but he only had a grade five education, so he had to take only hard labour work."

"Dad was pretty young when you got married."

"He was too young," said Margaret, "just turned twenty but, you know, when you're young you don't always do the proper thing. I remember when we went to see Father McDonald about publishing the bans he told us we were making a mistake. Everybody knew there was gonna be a war soon and your father didn't have a steady job, so Father McDonald didn't want us to get married because too many things could happen, he said. Your father had a seasonal job working for the city then and he was pretty stubborn, and he told Father McDonald that it wasn't his business, and they started to argue. Your father didn't have a lot of schooling, but he was still pretty well informed about things, and he figured he'd be in the army in a few months. I was proud of him then."

She took a kleenex from a small packet and blew her nose. When she looked up, Alphonsus had disappeared down the hallway and into his room.

Mary Power was the only person that Alphonsus looked forward to seeing now on the job. Of course, she was too young for him, so he thought. She was barely nineteen years of age and just a year out of high school. She had been hired originally the previous summer as temporary help but when the busy summer period expired, Mary was kept on by the management. Her father had died in the spring of the year after a long illness, and her plans to attend college were put off for the time being.

87

Alphonsus thought her to be quite efficient. She usually asked questions when something stymied her.

She was petite, and winsome, and everyone seemed to perk up when she was around. Alphonsus had seldom indulged in loose talk with her, discussing little more than matters concerning the business of the hotel.

So he was surprised when she said to him, "There's writing on the back of your coat. I noticed it when you came in this morning."

She was standing in the doorway of his cubicle, dressed in a form-fitting tee-shirt and a simple skirt. A faint smile lit up her face.

"Oh, yeah?" responded Alphonsus. "Where? I didn't notice."

He swivelled his chair around and reached up to where his coat hung on the stand behind his desk.

"It says 'tax something,' I think," Mary said.

"No kidding."

Alphonsus spread his coat out on the desk, and written on the back were the words "Tax Evader."

"Holy Moses! I should have known," he said

"Oh, my goodness!" she laughed. "You've got to have a good sense of humour, but it's a little embarrassing to know that you've been walking around with that written on your coat."

"Oh, I don't mind. Those guys down at the bar are always fooling around. Don't worry. I'll get them back."

He began to wipe it off with his hand. It seemed to have been written with yellow chalk.

"Here, I'll wash it off," Mary said.

Before Alphonsus could protest, she had picked up the coat and walked out of the cubicle and away from the office area. When she returned with the coat, the printing had virtually been obliterated. She held it up to show him.

"I think it'll just completely disappear in time," she said.

"Well, thanks a million, Mary. You didn't have to do that. It's not part of your job description," said Alphonsus.

"It's no trouble," she said cheerfully, and returned to her desk and her work.

Alphonsus had intended to buy her lunch for quite some time, actually, as she was a great help to him around the office. But he had always put it off, mainly because of the difficulty he had communicating that kind of suggestion, and the fear that the other employees in the office would cast aspersions upon his intentions with such a young girl as Mary Power. He saw her latest act of thoughtfulness as an opportunity not to be missed. So he called to her to come into his office.

"I'd like to take you out to lunch today, Mary. Would you be interested?"

"I'd like that," she said, as if she had been expecting the invitation.

It was as simple as that. But he did not want the other employees to know that he was taking Mary to lunch.

"Could we meet somewhere then? I'd prefer it that way," Alphonsus suggested.

"Yes, of course."

They arranged to meet in front of the cinema on Côte de la Fabrique, a five-minute walk from the hotel. From there they walked together to a small restaurant which served a good and inexpensive "business" lunch.

Chez Tante Annette was a bustling eating place.

Alphonsus was a fairly frequent patron here, mainly because it gave him the isolation he thought he required from people he knew at the hotel.

They were met at the door by a buxom, middle-aged woman who smiled at Alphonsus in recognition.

"Deux seulement?" she asked.

"Oui, s'il vous plaît," he answered.

They were taken to a small table for two, one among many tables packed closely together. There was no thought of seclusion or privacy at this restaurant, the idea being to move as many people as possible in and out during the noon period. More like a brasserie or tavern than a cozy, quiet dining room. But the food was excellent, reasonably priced, and the atmosphere congenial.

"The lady knows you?" observed Mary.

"Yes, I'm pretty much a regular here," said Alphonsus.

They were seated close. Mary had her elbows on the table and leaned toward Alphonsus, her eyes looking eagerly about the restaurant, taking in the surroundings with considerable relish. That was a quality he liked in her. She was not timid, but adventuresome in spirit.

The waitress came and they ordered from the daily specials.

"You're still staying with your mother?" asked Alphonsus.

"Yes. We've lived in the house on Bougainville for almost ten years now."

"You have an older brother, right?"

"Yes. Francis. He's an officer in the army. He graduated from the Royal Military College in Kingston. He's at Camp Gagetown in New Brunswick now."

"How old would he be now?"

"He turned twenty-five last August."

"Well, I don't remember him in school. He would have been too young for me to know him."

"In what year did you graduate from high school?" she asked.

"Twenty years ago, last June," he admitted.

"Twenty years! But you look so young!" she said, touching him softly on the hand.

"Thank you, Mary. Tell me. How do you like it up at the hotel?" he asked.

"Oh, I really like it. You meet all sorts of people. I like taking the mail around. I walk a lot, you know. It's fun."

"Well, Mary. You do a great job."

Then the food was brought to them.

"We'd better eat up. We've got to be back soon," said Alphonsus.

He wondered what she saw in him, as he sensed a gleam of contentment in her face, sitting opposite him. After all, he must have seemed a mysterious character to her, a bachelor past his middle thirties, unpleasant for the most part at work. She no doubt had noticed him on "mornings after" while he was drying out, attempting to conceal his hangover under the guise of business-as-usual.

He'd always been passive toward her since she'd started working at the hotel. Perhaps she liked him because of that. Alphonsus had noticed how the male room clerks made frequent attempts to flirt with her, but it was difficult for them since he was the all-seeing presence in the front office desk area. She was probably impressed by his "maturity and quiet competence." These words had been used about Alphonsus in a letter of recommendation he had received from the newspaper where he was previously employed.

He saw himself walking lush, summer fields with her and basking in her arms beneath the wide branches of pine trees—if she would spend the time with him and get to see him at his best. He could love someone like her, unselfishly, forgetting his aberrations.

They walked back to the hotel, dallying before a few shop windows, half-running across streets between slow-moving cars in an early afternoon traffic jam. The colourful streets around the old city were bathed in invigorating November. It would have been nice not to have to go back to the office.

While crossing the last street before the hotel, he took her hand for the first time. Her response was quick and gratifying to him. She clenched his hand tightly, securely. However brief, it was a moment of reassurance for him. He, Alphonsus Kerwin, the "reprobate," cantering across the street with a sweet-looking, youthful girl, tittering as she ran. He suddenly wished he could be seen by some of his friends at Hogan's. They would certainly envy him now, the bastards!

While lying in his bed that night, he thought about Mary, listening to the strains of Irish harp music, his mind then drifting back to an experience he had had with a young female cousin at his uncle's farm. Many of his mother's relatives lived north of Quebec City in a community of farming people of Irish descent. As a boy, he'd been invited to spend a few weeks. The younger visitors would always be sent up to sleep on the second floor of the farmhouse, a wide and open area, roughly finished with several beds and bunks spread about at random, which reminded him of the loft in the barn.

One morning, as he awoke to the sun's rays streaming their brilliance across the room, there she stood,

Mary Ann, second cousin, thirteen years old like him, staring down at him as he lay across the rude bunk, he clad only in jockey shorts against the heat, his phallus fully extended, bulging grotesquely at the front of his underwear. When he realized what she was gaping at, he quickly grabbed at a blanket lying at the foot of the bunk and covered his vulnerable area.

"What the hell are you staring at?" he hissed at her.

"Don't worry," she whispered. "I know what happens to boys."

She then had the gumption to sit down at the side of his bunk and grin and look him over. Soon she had calmed him down, the brat, and suggested that she lie on top of him. In his curiosity he was not about to refuse, and she stretched out her long, thin body on top of him and he just lay there under her, staring at the ceiling.

He did not even put his arms around her, and his manhood soon reverted to normal with the insignificance of it all. Yet he loved the closeness of Mary Ann, and they repeated the procedure a few times more during the time they were together at the farm.

"This is what my mom and dad do," she would say.

They would walk through the golden hay-filled fields of radiant July, hiding from each other amid the tall, multiple strands of grain that they would eventually tramp down into the hay wagon with their Uncle Willie calling out, "Look out for the fork now, kids!" as he pitched large forkfuls of hay up onto the wagon. Then Mary Ann and he would sneak away and walk together to the edge of the hay and oat section to where the trees, birch and pine and balsam, began to mass into the verdant multi-shaded heights of growth. Here, in the thick moss, they would stretch out on their backs in all their innocence and look up at the white clouds slowly weaving their configurations across the blue sky.

"I can see an old man's face. He's got a long beard," Mary Ann would say, sitting up and staring at one particular grouping of angel-hair clouds.

"I can see a weird-looking creature snarling," he would answer, pointing to another arrangement of cumulus.

When, in his arousal and wonder, he would touch her hand or her short auburn hair, she would look at him, unsmiling, and pull herself away, or jump up and start running across the carpet of moss, then stoop, and pick and eat the multitudinous blueberries, even the white and pink unripened ones.

She'd been tall and slim, as he was, and she ran like a deer, faster than he, and he'd told her that even if she was faster in a short race, he would eventually wear her down and catch up to her in the longer course.

One day they decided to put his statement to the test and he took after her across the barnyard and out into the field of hay that he knew his Uncle Willie did not want trampled. She then ran along the edge of the fields where the trees began, well ahead of him, about a quarter of a mile from where they had started. She began to giggle then and scampered into the taller tree area, and soon he was chasing her in and out and around brush and bramble. She was, indeed, beginning to run out of steam and he could tell that he would soon catch up to her, but the contest had ceased to be a joke and he already had several welts and scratches from the sharp limbs and shoots. When, finally, he reached out to grab hold of her, she fell, and he fell over her body, but he hung onto the back of her blouse, ripping it, and they both lay on the cool, red earth below the branches of a soft-needled pine tree. Totally exhausted, both of them breathing labouriously, they eyed each other.

"You tore my blouse!" she managed to say, between heaves.

"I'm sorry," he wheezed.

But she was angry at him for having caught her. She slapped his hand away from her torn garment and sat up, composing herself.

"Well?" he teased after a few moments. "Didn't I tell you that I would catch you?"

"It's because I started to laugh."

They lay on the cool earth below the pine tree cushioned with the dropped needles of decades, where the sun no longer reached, and he leaned over and touched her lips with his, only briefly. She stood up then, still a mite frustrated, and walked back out toward the open meadow. He caught up to her and she allowed him to hold her hand as they trudged back to supper under a cloudy sky.

And she smelled of timothy and dewy grass and he longed for the morning when she might come to his bed and lie on him.

But when she took the bus back to Montreal where she lived, although he expected that she would throw her arms around him at the bus station and wail and embarrass him in front of his aunt and uncle and cousins, she hardly seemed to notice him, hardly said goodbye to him.

So he went back to Quebec City and Champlain Street broken-hearted, devastated that she had not kissed him goodbye, and when he would hear the boats whistle on the river at night, he wondered if he should write to her . . .

Feeling some guilt because of his episode with Mary Ann, he went to the old church, St. Patrick's, to make his peace with God. One priest was hearing confessions and as Alphonsus stood in line with half a dozen other penitents, the frightfulness of lust was forever made clear to him. In the deathly quiet of that line, where he could hear the breathing of at least two other people, the words of ancient Father Kiley rasped out from inside the confessional box.

"How could you do such a thing? Didn't you realize that this could cast you into the fires of everlasting damnation? Do you realize how serious adultery is in the eyes of God? And this is not the first time, you tell me! How can I possibly give you absolution? You will just go out and see this woman again! Have you any idea of the hopelessness of the ravages of hell? Mind you, you've made Satan very happy! And you, a married man! With children, I suppose? Do you have children?"

"Yes," a subdued voice was heard.

"So you have children! How disgraceful, how utterly useless you are! Until you make a solemn promise to me that you will no longer seek the company of this Jezabel, I cannot give you absolution! Do you hear me? Good day!"

With that, the sliding window was heard to shut and after a brief moment of utter silence, a door on one side of the confessional opened and out stumbled an elderly man who would surely be in his seventies, head bowed, carrying a cane.

After being an inadvertent witness to this castigation, Alphonsus had wished with all his heart that he could be somewhere else, but he could not bring himself to abandon his position in the line-up. Besides, he was one of the altar boys at the church and most of the people knew him.

When his turn came, he gave old Father Kiley a mild story about how he kept fighting with his sister Katy, and how he verbally confronted his mother when his father wasn't around. He omitted once again to tell the devastating account of his impure thoughts about his cousin Mary Ann, a residue of his unclean acts with her the summer before, and how he could still feel her lying on top of him, her cheek pressed against his.

He never got into writing to her, and hardly ever saw her again. She eventually got married, then divorced, then remarried, and he lost track of where she was living.

* * *

Mary Power's home sat neatly on quiet Bougainville Avenue, a street made up of self-contained residences, many with ample front porches and compact lawns. When Alphonsus pressed on the buzzer, the door opened almost immediately and Mary's smiling face greeted him, together with a waft of warm scented air. Italian cooking.

The inside was immaculate, with soft lighting and attractive furniture. There were pictures of her deceased father on the wall, as well as coloured photos of her uniformed brother resting on a dark brown buffet, shining in front of full-length curtains at the front window.

She could change his life, this girl. She sat beside him on the chesterfield, her shoulder touching his, a faint, sweet perfume enveloping her.

"Mother! Alphonsus is here!" she called.

"Yes, I heard. I'll be right in," Mrs. Rob Power answered.

She was a short, portly woman. Alphonsus towered over her.

"Pleased to meet you, Mr. Kerwin," she said. She put out her hand and gave him a firm grip.

"It's a great pleasure," said Alphonsus.

"I hope you like lasagna," she said, "and you'll have to excuse me. I want to make sure everything is all right. I hope Mary doesn't give you too much trouble at the hotel."

"Oh, we only keep her because of her good looks," joked Alphonsus.

Mary laughed, but Mrs. Power looked at Alphonsus, just a little bewildered. Then she smiled.

"It should be ready in half an hour. And, Mary, did you offer Mr. Kerwin a glass of wine?'

Then Mrs. Power went back to the kitchen.

"Would you like a glass of wine?" Mary echoed, snickering.

"Would you have anything stronger?" Alphonsus wondered.

"Well, we have rum, vodka, and a little Scotch that's about five years old that Dad used to take."

"With all due respect, the Scotch will be fine."

"Do you take ginger ale in it or anything?"

"God forbid, no."

"Just some ice cubes, then?"

"Two will be fine. On the rocks, as they say."

She smiled again and left him. She was a beautiful young woman, dressed in a green tartan suit and white blouse. He felt somewhat out of place here under ideal circumstances, being served by two petite women, in a cozy environment.

"Bless us, O Lord, and these Thy gifts, which we are about to receive, through Christ, Our Lord, Amen. We always say grace, Mr. Kerwin, and I knew you'd have no objections."

"Of course not, Mrs. Power. It's a fine habit."

"And how long have you been at the hotel, Mr. Kerwin?"

"About a dozen years now, I guess," Alphonsus minimized.

"And how is the hotel business this time of year?"

"Well, it's pretty slack right now. The hotel has to be full if we're gonna make any money. So it slows down in November but it will pick up for the Christmas period and then, of course, during the Winter Carnival."

"It was hectic all summer," put in Mary.

"Yes, summertime is the peak period," said Alphonsus.

"And you get mostly Americans during the summer, I suppose?" said Mrs. Power.

"Oh, yes," agreed Alphonsus, "ninety percent. They're big spenders. They like to spend the Canadian dollar since, at this time, their dollar is worth more than ours."

"Go ahead. Just help yourselves now," invited Mrs. Power.

Mary served Alphonsus some lasagna from the casserole dish. There was wine, and salad in a side bowl.

"And I'd like to see Mary go to college next fall. She has a scholarship, you know," went on Mrs. Power.

"Oh? Is that so?" said Alphonsus, looking at Mary admiringly.

"Yes. Her father left her an insurance plan and they'll pay her tuition when she goes. I didn't want her to go this year because I wanted her to stay with me for a while. But I'd like to see her get a higher education. And don't you agree that it's a good idea, Mr. Kerwin?"

"Yes, certainly, Mrs. Power. Nowadays one must be more skilled than ever."

"I like the hotel business. It's an education in itself," said Mary.

"Yes, that's true, Mary," agreed Mrs. Power. "But with only a high school education you are not qualified to advance yourself. And don't you agree, Mr. Kerwin?"

"Yes, I have to agree, Mrs. Power,"

"And did you attend university, Mr. Kerwin?"

"No. I'm afraid not, Mrs. Power. There wasn't much money around for that where I lived."

"Alphonsus has done very well. He's a manager up at the hotel," said Mary, defending him.

"I'm not the manager of the hotel, Mary. I'm just the front office manager," said Alphonsus.

"Well, you have a very important job. You seem to run everything at the hotel. At least that's how it looks to me."

"Boileau is the real manager. He runs the whole operation. I just sort of take care of the guests and their accommodations."

After the meal, the three of them moved back into the living room area, Mrs. Power talking about her son in the army and about the last months of agony leading to the death of her husband, how he had steadily lost weight as a result of lung cancer, later developing brain tumors, taking chemotherapy, and losing all of his hair.

"He was just a skeleton when he died. It was such a terrible thing and they tried everything to keep him alive, but nothing could pick him up. He turned brown . . ." she went on, ". . . I'm sorry, Mr. Kerwin. I shouldn't burden you with this. But it seems just like yesterday and yet it seemed to take an eternity for him to die."

"My mother tends to get depressed," said Mary, after Mrs. Power had retired to her bedroom for the evening.

The stillness of the house impressed him.

"It's very quiet here," he said.

"Would you like to see the playroom downstairs?"

"No, not really. We'd disturb your mother."

"No, no. Come on. We'll be silent as lambs."

She told him to remove his shoes, took his hand, and led him down.

"This is really what I wanted you to see," she said. "My dad did all the work down here."

Spread out before them was a comfortable sitting room with brown-walled panelling, a billiard table, a television set. Built into one end of the lengthy room was a closed-off area with all the tools of the carpenter's trade impeccably ranged on shelves or hanging from hooks against the wall. An elaborate lighting arrangement gave the basement a luxurious aura.

Mary was misty-eyed, softly saying, "Dad's hobby was carpentry. He spent a lot of time down here. Mom makes sure everything is kept clean. She even dusts off the tools and things. It's almost as if she expects him to come downstairs and start working at something."

"But enough of that. Would you have another drink?" she asked him.

"Only if you will."

"Okay, I'll have some more wine."

"I'll have more of that Scotch on the rocks."

This tops suite service at the hotel, thought Alphonsus. He allowed his head to sink back onto the soft back of the sofa and closed his eyes, enjoying the stillness of the basement.

"Alphonsus! You're not going to fall asleep on me now!"

She was back from upstairs with the drinks.

He sipped on the Scotch, put his arm around her, and she snuggled against him, fingering his necktie.

"It's funny to hear my mother call you Mr. Kerwin."

"I guess she thinks I'm robbing the cradle."

"No, not at all. I think she respects you. After all, you are my boss."

"Maybe she didn't expect you to invite such an old guy to dinner."

"Come on, Alphonsus. You're not that old. My mom was in her thirties when she got married. Didn't I tell you?"

"I guess you did."

"She was older than my dad."

He kissed her on the forehead, pressing her face to his. She smelled so good. Mary put her wine glass down on the coffee table before them. She took his hand and brought it up to her mouth and kissed it.

"You have gorgeous hands. I love your hands, Alphonsus."

"You love my hands, eh?"

She giggled. "Why? Do you think that strange?"

"No. It's just a compliment that I've never heard, that's all."

"Well, your hands are so athletic looking. They're like a working man's hands, except they're so clean. I mean, your hands look as if they're used a lot. Does that sound strange?"

"Nothing you say sounds strange, Mary. But what about my face? Do you find my face as attractive as my hands?"

"That's funny. I've never noticed your face. Just your hands."

They both laughed. She stood up and turned on the stereo. Soft music. Strings.

"Would you like to dance with me, please, Mr. Kerwin, sir?"

"I'm not a dancer, Mary. But for you, I'll do anything."

They danced together to the slow sentimental music, she pressing her slender body to his, her hand fingering the back of his neck. His lips touched the top of her ear.

Cecile was more formal when she danced with him, he thought, when she could get him to dance at all. Wouldn't she like to see him now with this young chick, giving herself to him.

When the music ended, Mary looked up at him, tentative, willing to exchange a kiss, but he pecked her on the nose, let go of her, picked up his glass, and sat down to sip on his Scotch.

Actually, she'd come on to him a little bit too fast, he thought.

He could understand her mother's concern. Mary appeared willing to give herself to him without much persuasion. She had a child's comprehension of love, a vulnerable acquiescence. He probably could have laid her right there on the chesterfield. She was, after all, a woman, too. He could see himself unzipping his pants and trying to get himself into a suitable position to make love to her. What a mess that would be! But there, in that hallowed house of pain, where her father had succumbed, was no place for him to indulge his base appetites. It would be sacrilegious, the lowest of the low, gluttony and debauchery.

Yet she had stood there, pleading with her eyes for him to covet her. If he would only use his athletic hands to explore her.

"I hope you enjoyed your evening," she said to him, helping him on with his coat at the doorway.

"Yes, it was just marvellous."

He kissed her lightly on the forehead and opened the door.

"I'll see you Monday," he said, and walked away.

Alphonsus took the city bus down to La Grande Hermine, a bar he frequented on occasion, went in, sat on a stool, and ordered a double Scotch. The bar was relatively quiet for a Saturday night, and he sat looking at the golden liquid embedded in the ice cubes, transfixed, at a loss as to what he should do about his romantic attachments.

When he left the bar to walk home across the dark Plains of Abraham, he decided to drop into the Café Canton, which featured "Mets chinois," to wish kind regards to Sam Wong, his old buddy.

Over the years, he had been a late-night client of the restaurant, usually visiting it for some chicken fried rice and noodles.

As he entered the small eatery, little Sam was already involved with an apparently irate customer who glowered at Sam and was shouting obscenities in French. A young woman companion tugged at the large man's sleeve, begging him to return to his seat. Alphonsus stood in the aisle between the rows of small, delicate tables, motionless, as if impaled by the intensity of the large man's anger. Alphonsus was really waiting for Sam Wong to turn his attention to him. He was rather awkwardly posted close by, as if to interfere, which he originally had absolutely no intention of doing.

"What's the trouble, Sam?" Alphonsus then heard himself say.

"Oh, him not pay bill last time!" said Sam Wong, waving a single bill of fare.

The use of English seemed to inject renewed fury into the eyes of the large man.

"What the fuck you want? This is not your business!" he said, his voice full of indignation at the effrontery of Alphonsus.

"Sam says you forgot to pay your bill last time. I know it's none of my business. I'm just translating." Alphonsus tried to be mild, but business-like. The Scotches he'd drunk had given him a rather carefree affectation.

"I know what he said. I don't need no fuckin' translator!"

"I'm just trying to help."

Not as tall as Alphonsus, the man, in a light grey suit, must have outweighed both Sam Wong and Alphonsus by fifty pounds.

In no time, he had Alphonsus by the lapels of his jacket and was pushing him back toward the entrance of the restaurant. His face was cocksure. Alphonsus did not overly resist the current of pressure that was slow but constant. He was rather distressed that this two-hundred-and-seventy-five-pound offensive guard might take a swing at him. He could feel his sensitive jaw area already throb at the imminent blow.

As it turned out, Alphonsus was relieved that the entrance door of the Café Canton opened outwardly. For when they reached the entrance, the offensive guard simply gave Alphonsus a mighty shove which propelled Alphonsus out the door and down the three steps where he unceremoniously ended up in a heap in the slosh of snow on the sidewalk.

Alphonsus had had his eyeglasses on during the incident and now when he rose to his feet to shave the wet, gritty snow from his clothes, he saw his glasses lying, askew, on the sidewalk. As the large man stood inside the doorway of the Café Canton, glaring at Alphonsus and daring him to attempt entrance again, it occurred to Alphonsus that there must be a morsel of kindness in the big pecker. He could have smashed Alphonsus' glasses clean through his eyes, could he not have?

Alphonsus straightened out the glasses as best he could and walked up the street away from the Café Canton. Anyway, the lenses were not broken. He would wish Sam Wong kind regards some other time.

*   *   *

Alphonsus feels like an actor in a mid-afternoon soap opera, knocking on another door, his rap answered by a lovely mature woman who gazes up at him, her face resplendent, seductively dressed in a low-cut, light yellow dress, the pink swell of her breasts so inviting.

A gentle fragrance of flowers pervades the apartment where Cecile lives. They are alone in the dwelling, her parents having gone out to a concert at the Arts Centre. He likes it that way, always having felt uncomfortable in the presence of Cecile's mother.

She takes his jacket and scarf, bids him sit down, and goes into the hallway to hang up his clothes. The windows of the apartment are large and a glimpse outside from his high-rise vantage point reveals a pattern of street lights latticed into a golden configuration stretching away to a glittering horizon.

She returns and sits down beside him, her nearness immediately giving forth a mild perfumed sweetness that he has always loved. He is happy to see her again. First he must apologize to her for his outrageous behavior of last week. He has buoyed himself up to do so, having had several Scotches at the Grand Hermine bar on his way up to their appointment. Somehow, he senses an affability toward her. She is over thirty years old so he does not feel that he is robbing the cradle. She is slim, elegantly tall-ish, and has beautiful features. She sits erect beside him and coyly slides her hand into his and begins to fondle his fingers.

"What happened to your eye?" she asks.

"Oh, nothing. Just a small accident."

He will not discuss it, surely not.

He is dressed for the occasion in his best suit, hav-ing showered and changed at the hotel in one of the vacant rooms before leaving. He wanted to put on his best front for her. After all, he was a guest in her home.

Cecile feels that it is good to be with him again. His long legs and arms amuse her so. Apart from a fairly ample stomach, he is slender. His face is sharply chiselled and the glasses he sometimes wears make him look like an academic. His eyes are blue and they exude intelli-gence, and his hair is full and neatly combed, as usual. They could have beautiful children together, she thinks suddenly.

"You're very quiet tonight," she says.

"I'd like to say how sorry I am for the way I treated you last week," he says, eyes downcast.

"All right. But I think it's more a case of misunder-standing, Al."

"Well, I certainly didn't give you much time to react."

"It's all right, Al."

She puts her arms around his chest and squeezes as hard as she can, then kisses his cheek. He turns her around and cradles her in his arms, bringing her face up to his, and begins to kiss her, softly at first. Her breath is fresh and sweet. He prays that his is at least adequate.

Alphonsus realizes that he is very hungry, not having eaten a bite since noon. He also needs to relieve himself. She takes his face in her hands and gives him a deep, meaningful kiss. That's it. Now Alphonsus must see the man about the horse.

Heading for the washroom, he removes his suit coat and hangs it beside his winter jacket in the hall closet. Then, while relieving himself, he wonders how he can induce her to offer him a drink. It's quite possible that she has nary a drop in the house. He notices that his manhood is already swelling in anticipation. Not for the drink, he hopes. Could this be the night? he wonders. Maybe she wants me to. She's not a child. Actually he has not been too forthcoming since he's known her, as far as sex is concerned.

"God, am I ready for this?" he says aloud. "Can my body take it?"

He hears the telephone ring, and as he emerges from the bathroom, Cecile is just replacing the receiver on the hook.

"My mother wants to know if she left the oven on. The concert is just getting under way. I think she suspects that I have a visitor tonight."

"So they're into classical music?"

"Yes, my father got some free tickets."

He kisses her on the cheek and they walk back to the sofa together, holding hands. Alphonsus feels the softness of her skin under the sheer fabric of her dress. It rather excites him.

"Do you have anything to drink?" Alphonsus tries to make the question sound as passive as possible.

"I have some Amaretto."

"Amaretto?"

"It's a liqueur."

"Oh yes, of course," He likes sweet liqueurs, in limited amounts. But if there's nothing else . . . "All right," he says.

She gets up, goes to the buffet, and retrieves the Amaretto from one of the lower shelves. She pours the liqueur into small shot-sized glasses. She returns to the sofa and places the drinks on the coffee table before them.

"We could afford to have a nice place," she says.

"Yes, I suppose we could."

They are looking into each other's eyes again, engrossed.

"Do you think we could do it, Al?"

"You mean tonight?"

She laughs and kisses him. Of course, she means could she and he make it together as husband and wife. But of course they could. He doesn't give it that much thought. He's much more preoccupied with what he has before him tonight. After all, Cecile is a fully grown woman with experience, warmth, and beauty. Better that he should save himself for her, a girl he met under truly romantic circumstances, well suited to him.

"Perhaps we could go out together and look for an apartment, or maybe a nice flat somewhere," she says.

"You have to plan these things ahead of time, you know, Al."

"Yes, preferably in the old part of town."

He is kissing her shoulders and her upper chest where her breasts begin to slope into fullness.

"Come into my room," she whispers.

He follows her out of the living room, down the hallway and into her bedroom, delicately lit, surprisingly spacious, with large oil paintings tastefully decorating the walls, a teak bookcase filled with volumes, a large desk, and a three-quarter bed.

She closes the door. Alphonsus stands beside the bed, his stomach churning, probably disintegrating into small fragments, smithereens. It is deathly quiet. He can hear his heart pounding.

"Are you all right, Al?" she laughs.

"Yes, I'm fine."

She contorts her arms around easily and undoes the back of her dress, kicks off her shoes, and allows the dress to slide down her body, then nimbly steps out of it. She is standing on the opposite side of the bed from Alphonsus, clad only in a sort of half-bra and a dainty little pair of panties with miniscule red flowers imprinted.

He snatches at his necktie, trying not to choke himself as he pulls the knot free, and proceeds to unbutton his shirt. She comes around the bed toward him, smiling, her pale red lips slightly parted, looking as lithe as a cheetah.

His legs progressively weaken. He will soon have to sit down. She prods him to disrobe, helping to unbutton the rest of his shirt, stooping down to untie his shoelaces, holding him up while he removes his trousers.

They sit on the edge of the bed, still with their underwear on. Alphonsus then lies on his back on the bed.

"Come, Cecile, and lie down on top of me," he says.

"On top of you? All right."

She stretches out on the length of his body, her cheek resting on his. Surprisingly light, she is, thinks Alphonsus. It is Mary Ann all over again for him.

"Put your arms around me, Al."

"In a minute. Just lie there, little darling," he says in English.

They lie still, for several minutes. Then the telephone begins to ring.

"Don't answer it," says Alphonsus.

They wait, and it keeps ringing. She jumps up then, goes out the bedroom door, closing it again. The ringing stops, and Alphonsus lies on the bed. It seems to him that he hears her voice, raised, angry, almost shrieking. Then, stillness. He gets up, pulls on his trousers, opens the door, and there she is, sitting on the small stool beside the telephone, her face in her hands, whimpering.

"What is it?" he says, resting his hands on her bare shoulders.

"It's that son of a bitch. He won't leave me alone!"

"Who? Who?"

"It's Jean-Charles, the guy I told you about."

"He sure picks his moments."

Alphonsus massages her shoulders. He bends down and kisses her hair, but she does not respond. Rather, she seems to grow sullen.

"Don't worry about it, honey," says Alphonsus.

He returns to her bedroom and dresses again.

* * *

When he left Cecile later that night and walked back toward La Grande Hermine, he stopped at Sam Wong's Chinese restaurant and had a plate of fried rice and noodles. He meant to ask Sam about the eventual results of the altercation that he had been implicated in, but since the restaurant was so busy he didn't get a chance to talk to Sam for more than a second.

The very next day at noontime, just as Alphonsus returned from his lunch break, Mary Power was waiting for him at the entrance of his cubicle.

"There's a man who wants to speak to you," she said. "He's sitting on one of the sofas in the lobby. You can see him from here."

She pointed to a man in a light-coloured coat whose back was turned to them.

"Did he mention his name?" asked Alphonsus.

"No. He asked for Mr. Kerwin in English. I told him you'd be back so he said he'd wait."

Alphonsus had no idea who it might be. People who did business with the hotel did not ordinarily deal with him, but rather with Manager Boileau or the Assistant Manager.

He approached the man. "I'm Alphonsus Kerwin. Can I help you?"

The man stood up, but did not offer his hand.

"Yes, my name is Jean-Charles Paradis. I wonder if I could have a word with you."

He was a shortish man, had a receding hairline, and was quite stocky with a fairly thick athletic neck.

"Yes, of course. What about?"

"I'm a friend of Cecile Martin. You know her, of course?"

"Yes, certainly, I do. Would you like to have a drink

of something? Or perhaps we could step into the coffee shop just here?"

Alphonsus recognized that this was Cecile's ex-boyfriend. He led the way down the lobby to the coffee shop restaurant and invited Jean-Charles to take one of the booths. They sat, facing each other.

"Can I offer you something?" asked Alphonsus. He wasn't going to suffer this fool gladly, but be must act as if he had some class.

"Just a coffee will be fine," said Jean-Charles.

Alphonsus got up and went to the lunch counter and got one of the waitresses to give him two cups of coffee, together with containers of sugar and cream, and carried everything back to the booth on a small tray.

"Yes, well, what about Cecile?" began Alphonsus, after he had settled down again.

"I understand that you have been seeing her," said Jean-Charles.

His English was somewhat accented, but otherwise seemed to come easily to him.

"Well, yes. I met her last summer. She has mentioned you a few times to the effect that you went out together for a few years."

"We went together for quite a few years. I plan to marry Cecile and I would like you to stop seeing her."

Alphonsus chuckled, but unconvincingly.

"Well now, wait a minute, Mr. Paradis. I've just seen Cecile recently and I assure you that she has no plans of that sort."

The man is in earnest, thought Alphonsus. There is a desperate look in his eyes.

"Mr. Kerwin, I have given my life to this girl."

"But what about her? Doesn't she have some say in this?"

"Cecile is going through a difficult time. She is not the right person for you. You do not have the same language or culture as she. She is not your type of woman."

"I believe that all's fair in love and war, Monsieur Paradis. If she chooses to spend her time with me, that's her business."

But Jean-Charles would not be allayed.

"Cecile is just fooling around with you," said Jean-Charles Paradis, "and using you as a pawn to make me jealous. Well, she is succeeding. I am a jealous person by nature."

"I'm sorry to hear that. It's too bad we couldn't settle this matter in an unbiased fashion. I mean, there are lots of fish in the sea. It seems to me that you've given Cecile your best shot and you've been found wanting—as far as Cecile is concerned, at least."

Hold on, Alphonsus! Don't antagonize the bastard too much!

"We have had some difficulties, Mr. Kerwin, but I believe I know what is best for her. On the other hand, what can you give her? Her parents are against Cecile getting involved with an anglophone, so you'll be saving yourself a lot of trouble."

"Really, Mr. Paradis! You can't be serious! There are millions of people in the world who have become involved with a person of another language. I don't see what that has to do with your problem."

"It is not my problem! It is yours!"

Settle him down, Alphonsus.

"Well, I really don't see where this discussion is

going to get us. Why don't we just allow Cecile to choose? She is the one who must decide."

"Things were going just fine until you began to interfere. She is my fiancée. We have talked about marriage for years now. It is humiliating for me to use these arguments, but I have to do so, just to warn you of the gravity of my feelings. So I am telling you that I will take the steps necessary to keep her."

Jean-Charles got up from the booth then. He picked up his topcoat that he had set down on the seat.

"The next time our paths meet, I may not be as pleasant," he added.

Before Alphonsus could utter a word in rebuttal, Paradis was gone. So that was the little twirp that was pestering Cecile! Strange that he, Alphonsus Kerwin, should become embroiled in a three-sided conflict punctuated by threats and passion, with livid undertones of racism. Perhaps he should begin to carry a gun with him for self-protection. Who knows? The jealous lover might try to knock him off. He seemed dedicated enough to try. What an unusual exchange!

Business at the hotel had plummeted in November. Nevertheless, it was as if the unpredictable had occurred. The manager of the establishment, Justine Boileau, tended to regard his employees as excess baggage during these times. Boileau's presence was more evident around the front desk where Alphonsus was in charge. He was hobnnobbing with the cashiers more than usual and looking over the accounts of the registered guests.

During this perod of minimal activity at the hotel, Alphonsus sensed that it was the proper time to advise Boileau that he, Alphonsus, should have some time off.

"How long would you plan on being away?"

responded Boileau, seated at his desk and rocking precariously on his swivel chair.

"Well, I took ten days off at this time last year. I believe I'm owed over three weeks now, so I'd like to take it all. I'd like to take a trip somewhere."

"Oh, yes? Where do you plan on travelling?"

"Possibly down south. Nassau, perhaps, or Jamaica."

Boileau swivelled while Alphonsus talked, the chair creaking menacingly. Alphonsus wondered how such a small chair, supporting such a large, corpulent body, could withstand the onslaught. He speculated as to whether he would be able to resist applauding wildly if the seemingly frail device which enabled the chair to manoeuvre would collapse, sending the lumpish Boileau crashing to the floor.

"I'd prefer it if you kept it to ten days or, at the most, two weeks. We've got the Bar Association convention coming up and then the preparations for the holiday season. You could take the rest of your time off after the New Year."

"I'm very tired, Mr. Boileau. I've been to see a physician just recently and his suggestion is that I need a long rest."

Boileau suddenly laughed, loudly.

"Excuse me, Alphonsus. But you sound like a burnt-out corporate executive, or perhaps it's the social aspect of your life that requires some letting up," he said, laughing again at his own sarcasm.

You ribald, raffish son-of-a-bitch, thought Alphonsus.

"No, I don't think it's that," chuckled Alphonsus, mildly.

Late that night, after another evening of drinking beer at Hogan's, he stumbled from the tavern and decided to walk the distance home. He wondered about himself and about how he could handle things from here on in. He thought about Cecile again and the sequence of events which had occurred earlier in the day. It dawned on him that she did not really know him, that she could never suspect the degree of detachment that he could feel for her. Already it seemed like weeks since he had last seen her, and not just a day ago.

Was he coming apart? Wasn't he the good-humoured freak who ran around the football field on sunny Saturday mornings in the autumn with his beer-drinking friends? Wasn't he the tall, good-looking "Anglais" that everyone at the hotel stared at as he walked through the lobby dressed in a snappy suit, holding a sheaf of papers, headed to somewhere important? Wasn't he Alphonsus Brendan Kerwin, wage earner and keeper of his mother Margaret, constricted by her arthritis, and of his sister Katherine, the hermitess whose fallacious view of self wallowed in sloth? Wasn't he the big stud, as perceived by Mary Power who was ready to surrender her vibrant young body to him? But most of all, wasn't he the "bard," as his friends sometimes called him, the maker of comical anecdotes who could provide the spark that could turn a cold winter evening into a romp at Hogan's tavern?

Yes, he was all of these, and he thought that he should remain so, as he walked across the bare, frozen expanse of park headed for the stairway which led down to the Cove. A crescent moon lit up the star-filled sky. The stubborn November wind tousled his hair and felt cold against his legs. It was time to put on the longjohns. He stopped at the head of the stairway and looked down at the lights along both sides of the river. He was more than half drunk and he relieved himself at the side of the stairway before he went down the rest of the way in the darkness.

"In Dublin's fair city, where the girls are so pretty," he sang, just as he reached the bottom, and he stood on Champlain Street, looking at the house where he lived, which was nearby.

This night he was able to go right into his room without disturbing anyone, so he lay on his bed, earphones tucked on, encircled by the Gaelic-sounding music of Vaughan Williams, the "Greensleeves" rendition reaching into his very soul, exuding golden visions. Disturbing, whimsical, and extravagant feelings chilled him, the music sweet, lamenting, and moving.

He reached to the small table that held a lamp beside his bed and opened a small book—an anthology of Irish poets. He read the poem "Song of Wandering Aengus" by Yeats, the strings of the Academy of St. Martin-in-the-Fields billowing and swirling through his head:

> "Though I am old with wandering
> Through hollow lands and hilly lands
> I will find out where she has gone
> And kiss her lips and take her hands
> And walk among long, dappled grass,
> And pluck till time and times are done,
> The silver apples of the moon,
> The golden apples of the sun."

He knew he would not be able to get to sleep easily. He didn't see how he could get things straightened away.

It was all too much of a hassle. He was not able to make a decision about what to do. It was all about his drinking, something he depended upon which enabled him to face his job and his circumstances and his apathy and his lethargy. How could he ever change to any serious degree? It would be better if he just kept on doing what he was doing and not involve himself needlessly with other people. Why spread the misery around? His sister Katy had him pretty well figured out.

"I'm a virgin and bloody proud of it," Alphonsus would say the next night, close to midnight, well into the quarts, loud enough to be heard by most of the clientele.

"Just what Canada needs, another thirty-seven-year-old virgin!" said Nick McConnel.

"That's sacred territory, you guys! Why don't you change the topic?" said Bill Hogan, passing their table with a tray of draft beer glasses.

"I'm a bachelor, Nick. I'm also a Catholic bachelor. I have a firm belief in the tenets of my religion."

"Ah! We've suddenly caught religion, have we? Since when have you become a religious man? Didn't I just hear you say a short while ago that you haven't seen the inside of a Catholic church in a decade?"

"That matters not one iota. I'm still a Catholic and a Christian. I have not become sexually permissive simply because it is in fashion to be so."

"Well, no one asked you to volunteer information about your private sexual life," interjected Pat Brennan.

"Well, I thought that since we're among friends that we could be candid."

"Your friend Slater is asleep," said Pat, pulling Ben Slater's hat down over his face as the latter's head sagged forward.

119

"Wake him up, you guys!" shouted Bill Hogan. "We're closing in a half-hour, and I don't wanna have to drag him out."

"If you're right, Nick, I feel sorry for the human race. No wonder we have syphillis and gonorrhea running rampant, what with everybody screwing around. We're into the Gomorrah Syndrome, that's what!"

"The Gomorrah Syndrome! What the hell is that?" cried Benny Slater.

"Read the Bible!" said Alphonsus, and with that he brusquely went for his topcoat and left the tavern.

He ignored the loud howls of laughter trailing him.

Once outside, he pulled his collar up around his neck, walked over to the taxi stand and got into the first car in the line.

"La Grande Hermine, s'il vous plait!" he said to the driver.

The Leaving

THE SLAVINS HAD BEEN FORTUNATE in acquiring the second-storey flat they occupied. The house they lived in faced the sprawling Plains of Abraham, a deeply historic stretch of Quebec City park, dotted with monuments, old artillery pieces, landmarks of The Battle, and trees. Lying on the south fringe of the old city, the park awkwardly presented the St. Lawrence River with a craggy and impressive precipice at the edge. On a clear late-spring morning, the sun would rise to be confronted with all of this—a merge of bright green foliage above the abrupt earth-brown declivity and the grey relic of the city in the background. The sun's rays flickered on the river flowing past the city in a giant sweeping curve.

Patrick Slavin dwelled here. He had moved his family from lower town over a dozen years back. This was a much better place to raise a family. When they had moved, rents were not easy to come by for a man with a large family, and he was not ashamed to say that he had prayed for such an environment, where his children could simply run across the street and have a front yard a mile long to play and run around in to their hearts' delight.

On this street facing the park there were, understandably, few places for rent. A very well-to-do class of people lived here, in aging but fashionably designed structures, worth well above what Paddy Slavin could afford in three lifetimes.

There were three "flats" in this three-storey house which, at one time, was owned and lived in by a seemingly wealthy man and his wife. He had died, and the widow, suddenly and surprisingly in need of revenue, had proceeded to divide the house into sections for rent. She was a Québécois woman, with whom Paddy got along superbly. She loved the brown-eyed children of the "Irlandais" and frequently invited them into the first floor section where she still lived, now with a sister. Paddy's hopeless French was a source of great exhilaration to her. While talking with him she continuously giggled, and Paddy well knew that the more he talked with her, the more he would continue to be in her favour.

But now, since the "accident" had wrecked his system, he saw less of her, just as he saw less of many of his great friends. He could still get around, but he could not stay on his feet for long. It was not that he would grow tired, but that his leg would begin to feel lifeless, and that horrifying numbness would begin in the back of his neck and head. When this happened he would have to sit down from sheer fright at what he could not understand was afflicting him. The doctors were a source of anger and frustration to him, for they did not seem to know what caused the numbness, or else they would not tell him.

"Since the accident, Mr. Slavin, the blood circulation in your leg has not been efficient," the young doctor from the Disability Board had said.

"But what about the numbness at the back of my neck?" Paddy would implore.

"Yes, I know," the doctor would answer, and then

would add evasively, "that poor circulation in your leg is bound to slightly affect the rest of you."

Slightly! Slightly! Thank God he could still make it to church, where he could consult with someone who knew exactly what was ailing him and what his destiny was.

Paddy had never been a person with a big social life, yet he was tortured by his real and certain inability to walk down to buddy Frank Savard's house for a beer or two, or to take the bus, on his own steam, to the country place where he'd been born and raised. He had always loved to visit, accompanied by his kids, in the Shannon and Valcartier area just north of Quebec City where many of his close relatives still lived. He loved to chew the fat with them about the days gone by. After all, he was not yet an old man. There should be some good years left in him.

"Still up, Daddy?"

From his rocking chair in the kitchen, Paddy had heard his eldest son Martin ascending the stairway.

"Yep. I think I'll hit the hay now. Just taking a few last puffs on me pipe." Paddy spoke jovially as always.

"Is Ma in bed? Is everyone in bed?"

It was after midnight.

"Yes, son. Where were you off to tonight?" He asked indirectly as if uninterested.

"Oh, I was just out with the guys."

"Did you go up to see Jim Grogan yet?"

"Who?"

Paddy knew of his son's difficulty in admitting his procrastinating nature, and his shyness at introducing himself. This was a typical youth feeling inadequate, luckless, and self-conscious. To a young person, the world outside appeared to be highly technical, beyond the reach of understanding and sensitivity.

The father relit the dimming ashes of his pipe, and rocked slightly in the only chair that was therapeutic to him. He looked up at his son standing at the kitchen door and wondered if the boy had been drinking. Martin then advanced with a sigh, pulled a chair from the kitchen table, and sat, not quite facing his father.

They were very much alike. The lifelong friends of Paddy had always stated that the resemblance was remarkable. The boy was taller, but lean and sinewy and handsome like Paddy. And the unstylish long-strided walk was identical. Paddy was proud of his boy, and he wished not to interfere with what he considered to be promising traits in the youth. Martin was intelligent, if somewhat shy, and already had an avid taste for reading and sport.

He spoke to his son, quietly.

"I told you to go up and ask for Jim Grogan at the hotel. Tell him who you are. He may have something for you. It won't hurt just to have a talk with him. Things are picking up these days at the hotel. The tourists are coming in. There should be lots of work of all kinds. Take anything, as long as you keep busy. Even if it's cleaning up at the tables or something like that. It'd be better than just hanging around with nothing to do. I've known Jim for a long time. Tell him who you are, like I said. He might find something for you up there. When I was younger, Jim's father often sent him out to the farm to help out with the chores. Good God, that must be over forty years ago."

Paddy's mind lapsed back momentarily into the memory of those days on his father's farm. A longing surged in him.

"I don't feel much like being a busboy," Martin protested. "I'd like to get into something that'd prepare me for college. I'm supposed to be a high school graduate soon. Cleaning up dirty dishes isn't exactly what I have in mind as a career."

"I know, Martin, I know. Maybe Jim can find a spot for you in the office up there. Who knows? But in case he doesn't have anything like that, I'm just saying that you can take something for the summer and make a few dollars to help pay for your college expenses. It's better than just loafing around all summer. You'll be finished high school in a few weeks, and you haven't killed yourself looking for a summer job."

He did not enjoy speaking sternly to his son, but it had to be done. The boy would have to take that initial step of asking for work.

"I haven't been loafing. I went down to the Unemployment Office. I had an interview with a guy down there. They told me they'd call me if they found something I could fit into."

"Well, that's fine, Martin. But sometimes it helps to know the right people. I'll call Jim and speak to him. He's got a big job up there and I'll just bet he can get you in there. That's what I'll do. I'll call him tomorrow. I think he goes to the twelve o'clock Mass all the time. I'll call him when he gets home."

With that, Paddy slowly and carefully got up from the rocking chair and went to the kitchen cupboard, and retrieved a bottle of rubbing liniment. Without speaking, he handed the bottle to Martin, who uncorked it, poured some of the burning scented liquid into the palm of his hand, and then with both hands began briskly massaging the back of his father's neck. This routine, which Paddy

125

insisted was the only therapy that relieved the numbness in his neck, was burdensome to Martin. He felt as if his hands were infringing the privacy of that taut, still muscular neck, now reddening from the friction of the rubbing. He performed the task when Paddy did not do it himself, but had deliberately evaded carrying out this duty on occasion. As far as Paddy felt, his son was the only one who could rub the liniment in with both smoothness and force.

"Are you still getting the pains in your chest, Daddy?" Martin had fretted over asking the question.

"No, son. I haven't had any of those pains lately. There's nothing wrong with me ticker. I'm not worried about that. It's just that damn feeling in the back of my neck."

"Why don't you go back to the doctor?"

"Oh, I don't think they're prepared to do anything about it."

Mary Slavin, the wife of Paddy, entered the kitchen clad in a nightgown, her feet dragging a pair of flappy slippers. At times her face showed a regretful look, as if she had just uncovered, in her mind, a dilemma of exasperating proportions. Paddy noted that she had that look about her now.

"Why don't you stop rubbing that stuff on your father? Can't you see it's not doing him any good?" She spoke softly but with a tinge of anger in her voice.

Breathing more quickly from the exercise, Martin went to the sink, ran some water over his hands, and dried them on a towel.

"'Night, Dad," Martin muttered as he left the kitchen.

Paying little heed to the unqualified advice of his spouse, Paddy continued rubbing his neck himself, then began to work his head and neck back and forth, sideways, and in a circular motion. He had gone through these calisthenics frequently, with courage, for it caused him some pain. And Mary would look at him cavorting, unable to hide her utter distaste for these exercises. But she did have pity for him now in his condition. He had been a strong and robust man at one time. All the years she had known him, he had been totally unafraid of hard physical work and he would never complain after arriving home to her in a semi-exhausted state after a long, hard day. Then he would sit down after his evening meal, his pipe dangling from his mouth, half asleep, spilling ashes on his lap. How many pairs of trousers had he ruined from this?

He was a good man, a religious man, and a loving and loyal father to his five children. She remembered the early years of their marriage, when work was not easy to find if a person was unskilled. Her man, who had not made it through high school, had always been able to find something to do, and she had never, since their marriage over twenty years ago, been put in a position where she had had to seek outside work. Now he sat there, frantically trying to revitalize himself, rubbing his neck and worrying and praying. She did not feel that he was being justly repaid for his wholly sincere devotion to his family.

Mary stood at the kitchen counter and fought to hold back tears. What had a man to do in order to enjoy the fruits of a hard-working and devoted life?

"Why don't you come to bed and stop doing that? You're only going to hurt yourself more."

"Good God, woman. I've got to try something. I just can't sit here and rot."

"The doctor told you to exercise your leg, not your neck,"

As oftentimes, he ignored the statement.

"Did you set the alarm for six-thirty?" he asked.

"Yes," she answered, and walked back to the bedroom.

Paddy was reluctant to go to bed, and it surprised him. He could not remember a time when he had not welcomed the peace of his bed, where after a moment the heat of his body would transfer to the sheets and covers, and a warm coziness would ease the tiredness from him. Lately, he'd been spending as little time as possible resting, for he did not want to miss the sight of his children coming into the house, their breathing a trifle heavier after play, smiles sent his way. Especially Bridget and Michael, the youngest ones. God had been good to him, in giving him such fine children who always seemed to be in good health.

Like the God-fearing "Irishman" that he was, the celibate in him had been difficult to overcome and, as a result, Paddy had not married young. Mary was fifteen years younger than he, in her mid-twenties, when she married him. The comfortable life that followed was, for Paddy, a desirable change. She was a hard-working, neat, and talkative woman, if somewhat nervous. The advent of the children into their lives represented great wonderment and contentment for them both. All of their five children bore the characteristics of both Paddy and Mary. They were witty, oversensitive, curious, and excitable.

But he had married too late in life, and fate had dealt Paddy a cruel blow. He was not a man prone to sickness, and it seemed that, since the misfortune of his accident, his run of good luck had come to an end. It was close to a year now that he was laid up. And he had been caught in this situation with his children still young, still needing him. Certainly the Company, through the Disability Board, had treated him fairly. All of his medical bills had been taken care of, of course, and the Company, through the Disability Insurance, still paid him, not a full salary, but the great percentage of it.

He could never, in his living days, forgive himself for the accident. Cockiness, not reckoning for his age's lack of litheness and suppleness, had proven him a fool. He remembered the mishap as if it had occurred yesterday. What an ass he had been in attempting to carry a load too heavy for him. He had been the Maintenance Supervisor in the large building where he worked and it was not expected of him to handle the "heavy stuff." Replacing windows was not one of his duties, but he would pitch in with Leo Genest and Frank Savard when the occasion demanded it. These men were the custodians of the building, and they usually handled the heavy work. But Paddy had always liked Frank Savard, and they aided each other constantly in various types of work in the large structure—a complex of offices, conference rooms, and small firms.

Paddy had gone over the gruesome, embarrassing, and almost comic details of the event a thousand times. It had taken place on the fourth floor in one of the offices of a law firm, where a half-dozen clerks worked incessantly on computers. There was a large window with a cracked frame to be replaced. These windows were larger than Paddy himself, so that a stepladder was needed for the task of removing and unhooking the upper part of the frame. They were old windows and had remained in use since the erection of the building some forty years before. Paddy had mounted the stepladder as the girls in the office had stopped working. They had stood in the doorway of the office to escape the cold breeze that would surely blow into the room as Paddy extracted the window. They had poked their faces out from behind the doorway, teasing him.

"Come on, Mr. Slavin. Let's see you handle that window like the tough Irishman that you are!"

They were always needling him, just as he kidded with them oftentimes.

He unlatched the hooks with the hammer taken from his overalls pocket, while halfway up the ladder. There was a loud squeal as he then pushed the window free, where it hung momentarily and precariously over the street below. Then he lifted it inside, clutching it by a vent in the center of the frame. God, those windows were heavy. They got heavier every year with the dampness soaked into them. He allowed the window to rest on the sill, which was just a few feet from the floor, while he caught his breath for a second. Then he began to lower the window to the floor, slowly so as not to cause a loud and harsh landing. While doing so, he also lowered his right foot one step of the ladder to get more leverage.

He missed the step!

And he was not more than three feet from the floor when it happened. Unwisely, he hung onto the window with all of his strength, as he fought wildly and clumsily for his balance. Then his foot hit the floor. A stabbing and excruciating volley of pain seemed to tear his leg from his body. The window naturally fell over him, unscathed. He had saved the god-damn window.

The first Sunday in June was hazy, clouding, and damp, yet this did not mean that the park across the street was inactive. A two-wheeled, horse-drawn rig calèche, laden with a few chilly tourists, moved along a smoothly paved road of the Plains of Abraham. The driver-guide babbled unceasingly and monotonously about the historic importance of here and there, which he carelessly pointed to with a short whip handle, still half asleep, hardly taking his eyes away from the rear end of the horse. With smiling interest, the tourists turned their heads from side to side, acknowledging what they were seeing now with their own eyes, unable to camouflage their utter fascination.

It was early in the season for the tourist business, and in the oncoming weeks the air would be warmer and drier, the foliage would be richer and more colourful, and the inhabitants of the old city would spill over, on hot humid Sunday afternoons, onto the grass of the park with their blankets, sandwiches, and children. For the old city was subject to an expanding and surmounting growth, and as the years had passed the tourists were increasingly likely to seek out places of interest at times when they would not be overrun by other tourists. As early as dawn on a morning in mid-summer, the beat of hoofs on the pavement was the first sound emanating from the park.

The first tingling sounds of morning came to him, at first fleeting, then shrill, in his drowsy awakening. Shielding his eyes with his hand, Paddy looked across the bedroom, past the rumpled form of his wife sleeping beside him, to the window, radiant, accepting the light of a new week. The morning sun's rays streamed into the room through the fleecy curtains, throwing patterns on the wall adjacent.

"O my God, I offer Thee all my prayers, works, and

sufferings of this day, in thanksgiving for Thy favours, in reparation for my offences," Paddy whispered.

A soft sound of footsteps was heard from above. Old Trottier was up for his early morning walk in the park. Soon he would descend the two flights of stairs, the only time he left his likewise elderly wife. Both pensioners, they occupied the flat above the Slavins, a smaller area, like an oversized attic, beneath the concave slanting roof.

Pushing the layers of covers off him, Paddy stiffly swung his legs out until his feet touched the floor. Then he sat up on the edge of the bed. He was sweating a little. Perhaps the time had come when he should change his long winter underwear for the lighter summer combinations he had in the bottom drawer of his dresser. Why not? It was already well into June. He could do this now. Naw, he'd change tomorrow. He didn't feel like running the bath this morning. He reached under the bed for his socks, carelessly crumpled inside his slippers, and heard creaks as his joints and muscles gave way with little protests of tired pain, a little pleasurable, evidence that he still had senses functioning. It strained him to get his socks on, his hands having to reach his feet, not knowing whether the socks were inside out or not, caring little as he pulled them on.

As he moved to stand erect there were more creaks. Six-twenty, showed the alarm clock on the side table. It would go off at six-thirty. He pressed the button down so that the alarm would not awaken Mary. He noticed himself in the mirror above the dresser, his underwear greyish, not standing quite as erect as he thought he was. Picking up his trousers hanging on the back of a chair, he saw the small burn stains of ash on the front legs around the crotch. And on his best pair of pants. He'd have to get a new pair one of these days.

Slowly, he moved down the hallway, slowly and on tiptoe by habit, so as not to awaken the others, toward the bathroom, cramped with the toiletries and towels necessary for his family, who were growing fast. While urinating, he felt a soreness in his mouth, a pain deep into his upper gums. This could not be caused by his teeth, he thought, for most of his uppers had been removed over the years, and a plate had been substituted. Perhaps what Mary had warned him about had happened—an irritation of the gums because he did not brush his plate often enough. He took out his upper plate and, using the small mirror from the shelf above the bathroom sink, he tilted his head back and examined his gums. Nothing but the darkish pinkness of the roof of his mouth. He replaced the dental plate, and the mysterious, slightly irritating throb continued.

In the kitchen, Paddy went about preparing his breakfast, a regular practice of his since he had been unable to return to work. The soreness in his mouth had vanished, alleviating his concern over it. He shouldn't let every little ache and pain bother him. A soft-boiled egg and a cup of tea and a piece of brown bread toasted he would have, as usual when he came to think of it. He sat down at the kitchen table, after placing a cup and saucer and a knife before him, and waited for the kettle to boil.

He felt good this morning. He would exercise his neck before the rest of the family got up for Mass. Right after eating he would light his pipe and have a few puffs. And he must call Jim Grogan this morning for Martin. Jim would be happy to hear from him.

The kids were in such good humour these days, with only a few weeks of school left—then two months of holidays.

Mary found him as she expected she would find him, his index finger still tightly locked into the handle of his tea cup, his face flattened straight down onto the table, the kettle on the electric stove boiling madly. She touched his face, pale and a little purplish, and already cold, and waited for tears to help her express her terrible emptiness.

Martin Slavin

I DECIDED TO LEAVE THE HOUSE early and walk down to the hotel, which would give me time to think about things a bit. It was really nice out this morning, so I took my suit coat off and loosened my tie as I walked along Grande Allée heading toward the hotel. Quebec City is quite beautiful in early summer with the sun shining on the older houses, some of them grey stone buildings with brightly framed windows. It's funny how you can get an appreciation for things when you're alone, just observing how the old trees blend in with the architecture of a place.

My dad would have loved a day like today. He enjoyed walking around the city and the park in the spring. I remember him taking me into Battlefield Park when I was a kid. He used to help me climb up on the old artillery replicas that were placed around the art museum on the Plains of Abraham. There were always loads of people traipsing around, usually with their kids.

The death of my dad two weeks ago sent shock waves through our own family and all the relatives, of course. My mom found him in the kitchen, sitting at the table, his face flattened down on the table's surface, his arms spread forward as if he was reaching for something. She suspected the worst, but telephoned for an ambulance anyway. Then she came into my bedroom and woke me up. She was crying and told me about Dad.

135

I couldn't believe it, and Mom and I just sat there in the kitchen next to him, until the emergency guys came in with one of those portable wheeled stretchers. They couldn't find a pulse or any sign of life and eventually laid him on his bed and called for a doctor to come and examine the body and sign some documents. Then the men from the funeral parlour came and took the body away.

My kid sisters took it pretty hard. They were all standing around the kitchen, hugging Mom and crying a lot. Michael, my younger brother, just sat there with a stoical look on his face, as if this was a temporary situation which would soon pass. He eventually broke down at the funeral parlour when he saw Dad lying in the coffin. Michael is just eleven and in grade five. Two of the girls, Nancy and Ellen, are a little bit older. Bridget is the baby of the family. She just turned nine.

I'm sort of like the father at the house now, even if I only had my eighteenth birthday last month. It's kinda sad to think about my dad being gone when his family is still so young.

"Are you gonna take Daddy's place now?" my kid brother Michael asked me the other day. He's got these dark eyes that look right through you. He's really an extraordinary kid. He pulls down A's all the time in school, and his teacher last year wanted him to skip a grade, but my dad didn't go for that.

"He's okay. He's got his books and his fiddle lessons. He's got no time to get bored," Dad said.

My dad hadn't worked for the last year, not since the accident he had at work. He broke his leg when he fell off a ladder and the leg never healed properly, and then he developed circulation problems with numbness in his neck and head and he got pretty depressed. It's all so strange, because my dad was really as strong as a horse just a few years ago. I used to arm wrestle with him at the kitchen table and he had these great arms full of rippling muscles.

When I got to the hotel this morning, I had an appointment to see Mr. James Grogan, who is one of the managers there. I couldn't remember ever having met him, although my dad told me that I had been introduced to him out in the country place, Shannon, where my dad had been raised. My dad had talked about Mr. Grogan a lot, and they had known each other from way back.

The Château Frontenac Hotel is a very busy place, with people going in and out of the lobby in packs. I was a little early for my appointment so I sat in one of the big chesterfields and watched the bellhops loading the suitcases onto these dollies. I felt a little intimidated about applying for a job at the hotel and wondered if I'd be able to find summer work there. Other than that the hotel is a cool place. You can just walk into that big lobby and sit down and nobody will bother you. There's so much action going on all the time.

At about five to ten I went over to the front desk and told one of the girls that I had an appointment with Mr. Grogan at ten. She came out from behind the counter and led me up a stairway off the main lobby to a hallway where the administration offices are. She told me to sit down and she went into one of the doorways that had a sign above it that read "Chef Steward." She was back out in a moment and smiled at me and said, "Mr. Grogan will see you shortly."

Then she turned and went back down the stairway. She looked familiar and I felt by the way she smiled at me that she must have known who I was. Most anglophones around Quebec City know each other or about each other's families because we're a minority and we meet at events connected with the churches or the schools.

Mr. James Grogan soon came out of his office and immediately extended his hand to me.

"You're Martin, right? Paddy Slavin's boy?" he said.

"Yes, sir," I said.

He shook my hand firmly.

"Come on in and sit down," he said.

I followed him into his office, a really large room which could easily have been a luxurious accommodation at one time. He sat behind a shiny reddish wooden desk and I sat on the opposite side facing him. On one side of the room two huge windows, running almost from floor to ceiling, gave a spectacular view of the Dufferin Terrace overlooking the St. Lawrence River.

Jim Grogan, as my dad had called him, was a slim man of medium height dressed in a dark blue suit.

"Well, Martin, what can I say? I'm sorry for your trouble regarding the loss of your dad. He was such a good fellow. He and I go back quite a few years. I'm a second or third cousin of your father . . . anyway, we all came from the same family originally. Your father was five or six years older than I am and I remember going out to Shannon and working on the hay with your grandfather, I guess that would be, and your dad was almost twenty years old then, but he was full of fun and we had some great times. I'll never forget till the day I die. How old was your dad, Martin?"

"He turned sixty-two last January."

"My goodness! Sixty-two! That's young, nowadays," he declared. "I'm sorry I couldn't get to the wake, Martin, but I was out of town. But I did get to his funeral. Such a crowd! Of course, all the relatives from Valcartier and Shannon will miss him a lot. He was such a character. And how is your mom doing, Martin?"

And Jim Grogan went on, talking about who he met at the funeral and who he hadn't seen in thirty years, and who had died without his knowledge and who was still alive. I didn't know some of the people he was talking about. But I appreciated his concern about my younger sisters and brother and my mom, naturally.

When we eventually got around to talking about work he told me that I actually had two choices, which was kind of amazing to hear. He said that the main dining room would need another busboy, and if I was interested my job would be to clear away soiled dishes and tidy up tables and reset them. I'd be sort of a waiter's assistant. I would be instructed as to what to do by the people in the main dining room.

He also said that the gift shop in the hotel lobby needed a sales clerk and he asked me if I was interested in that sort of job. I told him I wasn't sure and he picked up the phone and was connected to the manager of the gift shop.

"Hi, John. Look, you told me you were looking for someone to work in the shop," he said. "Well, I have a good-looking young fellow here, Martin Slavin. Can I send him down to see you? . . . Okay, okay, John. So I'll send him down in a minute."

So he put down the phone and said: "Martin, why don't you do down and see John Doré? He's in the gift shop right in the lobby there. He's a nice fellow, and whatever you decide you'd like to do, we'll have one of the girls give you the application forms and you can fill those out. Have you any experience with hotels, Martin?"

"No," I said, "but I worked at a youth camp the last two summers. I helped out in the kitchen with the meals for the campers, and I did lots of different kinds of work."

"Oh, great. Then you know what working with people is all about."

I liked Jim Grogan right away. You could tell that he was a pretty busy guy and a good talker, but he had that way about him that kind of relaxed you. Before I left his office he shook my hand and offered me sympathy once more, and he put his other hand on my shoulder and I guess he would have hugged me had I allowed him to.

So I went back down to the main lobby, found the "Boutique du Château" and was met by John Doré, a tall man with a moustache. We squeezed into a small room at the rear of the shop where he had a desk and he spoke to me about what my duties would be if I would be working there. There were two cash registers in the shop, and the girls would explain how everything worked, and I would be selling lots of postcards, souvenir trinkets, souvenir watches, hats, tee-shirts, and various other items usually found in such a store. He told me to keep a suit coat and tie on at all times.

He also asked me how my French was and if I could handle French clients in a friendly, affable manner. We spoke in French then for a while. I explained to him that I had done my elementary school entirely in French and that my mom spoke French to me on a regular basis, so I was pretty comfortable speaking French as long as everything was straightforward.

Then, "Mr. Grogan told me that you lost your father just recently. I'm very sorry to hear that and I offer you my deepest condolences."

"Thank you, Mr. Doré," I said, pleased and surprised that he had been told—probably just before I got there.

John Doré rummaged through his desk and found an application form which he told me to fill out on the small cluttered desk. After doing that, I was introduced to Madame Sylvie Côté, who was the lady-in-charge in the shop itself. There were also two girls who worked as clerks, one of them temporary, she being a student just hired for the holidays like me.

I was told that I was to start working on Monday morning at nine o'clock. It seemed to be a given that I had accepted the job. There were no complications. I just had to show up and start working. I was somewhat mystified at how easy it actually had all turned out.

My mom had counselled me pretty well in preparing me this morning, making sure my hair was neatly cut and seeing that my clothes were presentable. I'm also pretty sure that Mr. Jim Grogan played a big part in securing work for me at the hotel.

I was riding pretty high when I left the hotel, so I decided to take a walk up the boardwalk, a popular place for both tourists and local people. It was close to noon and already there were droves of people strolling and milling about. I've been up there quite a few times with some of the guys, including once with our history teacher, Mr. Collins, who talked about the war between the French and the English, fought more than two centuries ago.

I sat on one of the long benches in front of the railing which overlooks the river two hundred feet below.

The sun was quite warm, and my mind lapsed, and I started to imagine what it would be like selling tee-shirts to American tourists.

"So I hear you'll be working at the gift shop," a voice behind me said.

I turned and saw the girl who had shown me to Jim Grogan's office.

"Oh, hi," I said. "How did the news travel so fast?"

"Oh, Mitzy who works in the gift shop told me."

She was holding a colourful lunch packet, and came around and plunked herself down on the bench beside me.

"When the weather is nice, I like to eat my lunch out here. I hope you don't mind," she said.

"No, not at all. It's a free country," I said.

"Didn't you play basketball in the tournament at St. Pat's a few months ago?"

"Yeah, I played for St. Pat's."

"I remember you. Too bad you lost that last game, but you were beaten by the best team."

"Oh, you must be from Quebec High."

"Right."

"Oh, brother! That was a real squeaker. It could've gone either way."

"Yes, I know what it's like. I play for the girls' team."

"You're kidding me!"

"Oh, I know. You don't think I'm tall enough to play basketball, is that it?"

"No, no. I didn't mean it that way. I just meant that it's amazing that we're both nuts about basketball, that's all."

Her name is Tracy Goodfellow and she's as cute as a button. She was hired for the summer too, and she works at the front desk of the hotel handling the registration of guests. I'm sorta shy with girls. I've never had a steady girlfriend, and some of the guys consider me to be a bit of a nerd when it comes to dating. But my mom and dad would have frowned at the idea of me having a steady girlfriend while I was in high school. If it had ever happened, which it didn't, I would have had to keep it top secret. But with my two kid sisters just starting high school, there's no way I could have had a steady without them knowing about it.

During the winter, my buddies and I go skating quite often at the arena when we're not playing hockey. I've met quite a few French-speaking girls from some of the French high schools there. But that is another chapter in the "secret romantic life" of Martin Slavin.

One of the great things about Quebec City is that there's no English-speaking ghetto. The anglophone inhabitants of the city are spread out and live in many sectors intermingled with francophones. Since they're surrounded by French-speaking people, most anglos learn to speak French when they're young, playing with kids in their neighbourhood. I used to hang around with French-speaking kids a lot and play in the expansive Battlefield Park just across the street from where I live.

I couldn't have been more than eight years old when I first laid eyes upon a fair-haired smiling young playmate who lived close to the park in one of those walk-ups on Cartier Avenue. I can't even remember what she looked like, really, except that she was French-speaking and when she looked at me, bright-eyed and playful, she told me that she had seen me at the playground the day before. I don't recall her name, and the memory of her is very distant, but every now and then the wispy thought of her crosses my mind, and burns like a low flame.

She wanted me to be with her to run through the playground and then out into the "Park" to bound around the grassy hills. We even went to the old Parliament Buildings area and ran along the low walls, and then made our way up to the Citadel and walked along the tops of the battlement structures, some of them quite dangerous for young children. If my parents had found out about my meanderings, I would have been grounded for the rest of the summer.

I then can recall standing at the bottom of a long flight of stairs leading up to her family's flat, and her mother looking down at me, unsmiling and unwelcoming, and telling me that her daughter was gone to play elsewhere. I'd known her for just a few days and she just faded away and I never met her at the playground again. I ached to see her, but soon after I was told that she had moved away.

Sometimes when I'm walking down some street, either on a bright sparkling day or during a rainfall, and I see some young kids singing in the sun or splashing around in the puddles, I feel that I'm just a little kid again and I'm starting to sense that girls have a different way of doing things. Then I might hear a young girl's voice with that certain timbre, and it hits me like a thunderbolt, and the whole experience renews itself and I'm brought back to those few days I spent with her at the playground.

My dad left a little money and a group life-insurance policy when he died, and my mom says we can get along for a year or so. After that, my mom says she'll look for work. Because of her French-Canadian ancestry, my mom speaks and writes French very well, and since she's only in her mid-forties, she probably can find work easily.

The Unexpected

HE REACHES TOWARD the ringing alarm clock, stretching an arm to the small side table, pulling the overlying quilt away from his wife who is next to him. The radio station tunes itself in with the energetic voice of the regular morning talk-show host.

Edward Harris pulls himself up and sits on the edge of the queen-sized bed. He looks down at his protruding stomach. He'd meant to get up one half-hour earlier and begin a regimen of early-morning walking, something his GP had recommended. But when setting the alarm the previous night, he'd forgotten all about his plans. He promises himself that he will begin walking tomorrow morning.

When Edward Harris has completed his usual morning ritual of shaving, showering, and dressing, he walks into the kitchen. His wife, Diane, has just placed hot bacon and eggs neatly on a plate beside his toast and orange juice. Her timing is impeccable this morning. She is standing now, leaning her back against the kitchen counter, her arms folded in front of her. She looks a mite apprehensive in her long kimono. Their son, Eddie, is already seated at one side of the kitchen table, sipping on a cup of coffee, skimming the sports section of the Montreal *Gazette*.

Another radio is on in the kitchen, a reporter giving traffic reminders to the hordes of solitary drivers who will soon clog the arteries leading into Montreal.

145

"Will you be late tonight, Eddie?" says Diane to her son.

"I don't know. Lemme think . . . let's see, today is Wednesday," says Eddie, looking up.

"Because I'm taking the train into town this afternoon," Diane goes on. "I won't be back until after nine tonight. Shall I give you the key?"

"No, it's okay. I have a class at eight tonight. So I'll be home pretty late."

"I'd really like to have the car. There's a few things I'd like to pick up," Diane suggests to her husband.

Edward Harris does not look up.

"I'm sorry," he says, "but I'll need it all day today. You'll have to take the commuter. And get yourself your own key, Eddie, for God's sake."

"I did have one, but I can't find it," the younger Harris says, pushing back his chair and leaving the table.

He's a tallish, slim specimen with his father's looks. He goes to the small powder room near the front entrance of the house and works on his hair, smiling at himself in the mirror, exposing a bright line of teeth. As a second year student at Concordia University, he usually does his best to look presentable.

"I'll be waiting outside, Dad!" Eddie calls back to the kitchen.

"Is your lunch in your bag?" Diane says, almost shouting.

"Yeah. Thanks, Mom."

Eddie goes outside into the brilliant sunshine. He sits on one of the steps on the porch stairway, soaking up the rays.

Edward Harris and son drive to downtown Montreal together most mornings, depending upon Eddie's class schedule. Their home is a comfortable, three-bedroom bungalow on a tree-lined street close to one of the train stations. But since Edward Harris is a downtown bank manager with handy parking privileges, the practicality of the commuter is not a factor for him. Besides, he just likes driving his Volvo to work, providing, of course, that conditions are favourable.

On this particular Wednesday in mid-autumn, Highway 20, one of the main autoroutes into town, is in an annoying snarl. Three highway lanes of cars crawl along.

"Will I be able to have the car Friday night, Dad?" Eddie asks.

"Any special reason?"

"No. A bunch of us are going to the basketball game and I just thought I'd pick some of the guys up and make it easy for them."

"We'll see. How's school going?"

"Oh, all right, I guess."

They don't talk to each other for any length of time these days. There is a kind of gap between them. Edward Harris wonders how he can bridge their lack of communication, whatever the cause. He remembers when Eddie was younger and how they used to go to the Montreal Canadiens hockey games together. They'd yak all the way back in the car, revelling in what they'd seen, laughing about the fights on the ice. Things seemed to be so much more uncomplicated then. He just can't seem to get a conversation going with Eddie—something beyond words of greeting or departure. He finds this deeply frustrating and envies parents who seem to be able to engage their children in enjoyable and animated exchanges.

Edward Harris drops his son off on a street corner close to the university and joins the line-up of cars snaking along St. Catherine Street toward the commercial area where he works. He is going to be late again, setting a bad example for his employees. He'll have to get up earlier in the morning: the damn traffic situation is deteriorating day by day.

Upon reaching his destination, he quickly drives down to the basement of the business complex, parks, then walks up the inner stairwell and strides past several shops with interior entrances. As he reaches the bank, Georges Gaudreau, his uniformed security man, is already inside with keys to unlock the large glass doors of the mezzanine entrance.

Edward Harris goes down the short stairway back to street level and walks across the floor of the bank. He is greeted from all sides by his employees. He answers perfunctorily with a few "good mornings," hardly looking at anyone. He masks a slight embarrassment with a businesslike manner.

It is just after 9:00 a.m. The bank will open its doors to the public in less than an hour.

Right on the heels of Edward Harris as he opens the door of his own office is one of his subordinates, Francis Paquet. Paquet is one of the bank's loans officers who also oversees the work of the tellers and is considered Bank Manager Edward Harris's right-hand man.

"Good morning, Mr. Harris."

"Morning, Francis. What's up?"

"There was a call for you from head office about ten minutes ago. A Mr. Giroux?"

"Oh, yeah? He's one of the honchos over there. What the hell does he want, I wonder?"

"He wants you to call him ASAP."

Five minutes later, when Edward Harris gets off the phone, his "reflux disease" begins to act up. He reaches into his side suit-coat pocket, retrieves a packet of Tums, and pops two into his mouth. He is also vexed because incompetence has raised its ugly head. One of his bank's biggest depositors has gone to head office with a complaint instead of coming to him. It seems that a rather large amount of money has been wrongly deducted from the client's checking account on the previous Monday.

* * *

The two men sit in a nondescript gray Dodge, having plunked several coins into the parking meter. They are parked down and across the street from the Mercantile Bank of Canada on St. Catherine Street. It's a crisp October morning and there is no need to explain to anyone why they are both wearing gloves.

"See the guy at the door there?" says the older, lean man in the driver's seat.

"Yeah, with the uniform? Is he carrying anything, do you think?" asks the second man.

"No. They don't carry any weapons. He might have a cell phone on him, but just take it away from him."

"So I cover him and look after anyone who comes in."

"That's right. Now once again, don't forget to wait till I come in by the other door upstairs, from the mezzanine that we saw yesterday. I'm gonna close that door and put the wood on so nobody can come in. As soon as I get to the foot of the stairs, you pull the gun on the guard. Get it? Should I go over it again?"

"No, it's okay. I get it. But are you sure there's enough cash hanging around? I mean, banks are not what they used to be."

The younger man has a slight tremor in his voice.

"Lookit! Don't worry about that! That's my department, just do your job like I said. And remember, no shooting. We don't want trouble any more than they do. This shouldn't take more than two minutes."

* * *

Edward Harris is seated on his swivel chair. His desk is clear save for a few documents. He always makes a conscious effort to keep the top of his desk uncluttered.

Two of the bank's tellers are seated in straight-backed chairs at the other side of his desk. Francis Paquet, the overseer, stands beside the desk, fidgety.

"So . . . what happened here, Francis?" asks Edward Harris.

"It looks like it was just a random slip-up, sir. Mrs. Ellis here seems to have made a few typos and the $6500 was mistakenly deducted from Mr. Mancini's account."

"So, Mrs. Ellis . . . what's your first name?" asks Edward Harris.

"Janet, sir."

"Well, Janet. How long have you been with us?"

"Just two months, sir."

"She's been at the front with us for just a few weeks, Mr. Harris," interjects Gisèle Filion, a veteran teller.

"Now, listen, Janet," says Edward Harris firmly, "this time we caught the error easily, but another time it might not be so easy. So just be very careful with these account numbers. They have to be accurate at all times.

And don't be afraid to ask questions. Gisèle here has a lot of experience. All right? Thank you, girls."

The two women get up from their chairs and exit the office.

"So why didn't the asshole come right to us when he saw this?" Edward Harris says to Francis Paquet. "This reflects on us, you know."

"I don't know. Maybe he thought there was some sort of scam at the ATM. He also does a lot of his business through the machines, apparently."

"Okay, Francis. Keep an eye on the tellers. I think when they see people lined up, they rush things a little. Tell them to relax, for Christ's sake!"

"Sure, Mr. Harris."

"All right, Francis. Send Miss Arcand in."

As Edward Harris opens the right side drawer of his desk and retrieves several files, he feels a sharp and very localized dart of pain high in his chest on the right side. It is as if someone is pressing the sharp end of a pointed stick into his chest. A slight surge of fear envelops him but the pain soon subsides and he is left wondering. He should have this checked out with the doctor. It isn't the first time it's happened.

Elizabeth Arcand enters his office.

"Good morning, Elizabeth."

"Good morning, Mr. Harris."

At the sight of her he is able to suppress his fears. She is a petite woman in her late twenties, dressed immaculately in a dark blue pantsuit and white blouse. A thin silver-tinted chain graces her neck, subtly matching delicate pearl earrings. She has been working with Edward Harris for over six months now, and he has grown to appreciate her bright personality and professionalism. He is aware that Elizabeth is engaged to a McGill law faculty graduate who is presently articling with a Montreal firm. But this has not deterred him from creating certain images and fantasies about her, and about him and her together.

Elizabeth is bilingual and bicultural and handles all of Edward Harris's difficulties with French translation. She also organizes many of the savings and investment accounts of clients.

Edward Harris sees little need to coddle her through bank procedures and correspondence modus operandi. She has already proved herself to be independently competent. In most cases, she is left to handle situations on her own.

So after discussion on a few of the files, he looks at her.

"You're like a breath of fresh air around here, Elizabeth."

"Why, thank you, Mr. Harris," she answers ebulliently.

"That'll be all for now. Thank you, Elizabeth."

She gets up to leave his office and he watches her move away, his eyes taking in the black tresses of hair and the youthful lines of her figure.

It is slightly after 10:00 a.m. and the doors of the Mercantile Bank are now open to the public. Security man Georges Gaudreau, a bunch of keys dangling at his waist, walks back to his position at the main street-level entrance after unlocking the upper mezzanine doors. Several customers are already conducting business as Edward Harris emerges from his office.

The bright autumn sun streams shards of light through the long sheer curtains in front of the floor-to-ceiling windows. Most of the customers at this time of day are the pensioners, who seem to have an aversion to doing their banking at the ATM. They are already lined up, bank books at the ready, many of their faces familiar to him. Edward Harris usually enjoys taking a minute to survey the goings-on. He is proud of the manner with which his workers handle the public—cheerfully and with respect.. He encourages this attitude.

But this morning he is feeling anxious, for some unknown reason. He has not digested his breakfast very well, and feels as if there is a bulk in his stomach stirring in him the need to belch. Yet he cannot seem to accomplish it. Beads of sweat surface along the creases of his forehead. He takes a clean white cloth handkerchief from his pocket and wipes his brow, then turns to go back to his office.

"Everybody on the floor! Right now!"

A loud masculine voice pierces the drone of subdued talking. Edward Harris, about to enter his office, turns to see a tall, thin man wearing a winter toque and large sunglasses waving a handgun in the centre of the floor.

"Get down! I want everybody down on the floor! Sur le plancher! Tout le monde à terre!" The voice is even louder now, and more desperate.

There is also another voice of another man at the doorway, who has already pushed Georges Gaudreau down to his knees against the wall near the main entrance. He is also holding a weapon.

The dozen-or-so customers in the bank, several of them senior citizens, stare at the tall man with the gun in their midst, and do not react to his commands immediately. They stand, wide-eyed, mesmerized at this departure from normalcy. The armed man then grabs the last person in one of the line-ups, an elderly man, and forces him to the floor. The others, both men and women, retreat to the wall and ease themselves down, trying to make themselves as inconspicuous as possible. Some struggle to perform this manoeuvre, one they cannot accomplish with ease.

The man with the gun goes to the business wicket and relieves the three persons of their deposit packets, no doubt the receipts of the previous day's business. He handily drops the lucre into a canvas bag, which is hanging from his waist. He turns his attention to the tellers and the cubicles behind the main counter. He does not seem to notice Edward Harris, who is standing in front of his office door.

"Put your hands in front of you! I wanna see your hands!" shouts the man with the gun.

There are three women tellers posted at this time of the day at their respective wickets. Two of them are handling regular chequing accounts of ordinary depositors while the third teller takes care of small business accounts, many of which belong to local retailers.

"Open your cash drawers! All of you! I know you have keys! Unlock them!"

His shouts are shrill and threatening. He waves his gun toward the three tellers, and then suddenly, in a brazen act of recklessness, vaults over the counter, and points his gun at the head of Gisèle Filion, one of the tellers. She fumbles nervously with her keys to open her cash drawer, and is finally able to accomplish it. He quickly scoops the contents of the three cash drawers into the bag. He is shocked at the meagre number of bills in the tellers' cash boxes.

A half-dozen or so bank employees are standing at or near the main counter, excruciatingly anxious, and wanting this experience to be over. Edward Harris, who has been completely ignored by both bandits, remains at the doorway of his office as if spellbound. He is now feeling weakened, helpless, and cannot take a deep breath. The sharp pain has returned to his upper chest, and he is close to a state of panic. He cannot align his thoughts. Flashes of images race through his mind. He sees his wife Diane and then his son, and his daughter, who has married and moved away to British Columbia. He knows that he loves her and sees her, as a child, running in the knee-high growth of wild flowers on a sunlit afternoon, her brightly coloured skirt blowing in the breeze. She is laughing, and calling to him.

"Daddy! Daddy! You can't catch me!"

The visage of Edward Harris is ashen, and he is totally drained.

They are gone. An eerie silence envelops the space where a profound emotional assault has occurred. The bank employees self-consciously repossess their hands, and the bank customers seated on the floor begin to stir. The entire episode, explosive to the senses of all, has taken less than two minutes. Janet Ellis, one of the tellers, begins to weep and is immediately consoled by some of her co-workers.

The two toqued men in sunglasses have simply walked out of the main entrance of the bank and melted into the crowds of a busy mid-week thoroughfare. Georges Gaudreau re-enters the bank, saying that one of the bandits has headed into a subway entrance, but then he says that he is not certain. Police have been alerted and are on their way to the bank.

Edward Harris, one hand on his chest, has somehow stumbled into his office. He is sitting on his swivel chair, his face down on his arms. He feels that he is losing consciousness, that it is slowly ebbing away.

"Are you all right, Mr. Harris?"

It is the voice of Francis Paquet, who has bent down close to Edward Harris. The wheels of the swivel chair roll back, suddenly causing the stricken man to fall away from the desk, but Francis Paquet manages to grasp Edward Harris and ease him down onto the carpet.

"Help! I need help in here!" calls out Francis Paquet.

* * *

The yellow ambulance, lights flashing and siren wailing, works its way up the hilly streets to the Royal Victoria Hospital. The emergency technician has applied an oxygen mask to the face of Edward Harris, who is tucked in the stretcher-gurney. Edward Harris can see through the rear window of the ambulance. The buildings are racing by, and he catches glimpses of the reds, oranges, and yellows of the autumn trees. He can also sense the wheels of the vehicle racing below him. These are his fleeting and fading impressions.

At the emergency reception area of the hospital, he is immediately wheeled to a station where nurses take his blood pressure, hook him up to a monitor, and rig him up for an electrocardiogram. But Edward Harris is fading fast and soon there is no perceptible pulse, so a defibrillator is used by an intern to get his heart going again.

* * *

From her kitchen window on this sunny October morning, Diane Harris had watched the two men in her life
drive away. She'd cleared the breakfast dishes from the
table and placed them in the automatic dishwasher. Then
to the bedroom, where she'd tidied up and put on her
gym togs. Lily Cormier, as promised, had showed up at
around 9:00 a.m, and the two of them had gone down to
the basement playroom and had practised their Tai Chi
with the video. Lily and Diane are both slim enough and
intend to stay that way. This Chinese exercise is designed
to develop and maintain co-ordination and balance, as
well as fitness, and after some early naïve enthusiasm, the
two women have discovered that its slow deliberate
movements are surprisingly demanding. But they have
stuck to it, and are now into their second month of Tai
Chi.

After the forty-five minute workout, they sit on the
chairs back up in the kitchen, in a mild sweat, sipping
water.

"So, how's your Edward?" inquires Lily.

"Oh, he's uptight as usual," shrugs Diane. "You
know, he should be doing the Tai Chi, not us."

"Is he overweight, just a little?"

"Are you kidding? I'm sure he could lose thirty or
forty pounds. I worry about him. He says he has chest
pain."

"Phil had a stress test last month, on one of those
stair-masters. The doctor stopped it. He was worried that
Phil's heart rate was a bit too elevated. The doctor's got
him on Lopressor for high blood pressure. So Phil is taking his two little pink pills every day."

"Men are so pathetic, really. They're so keyed up all
the time."

"And how about us, Diane? How many pills are you taking every day?"

"Just two."

They both snicker.

Their conversation is interrupted by the ringing of the telephone. It is Diane's daughter Kathleen, who is calling from Kelowna, British Columbia. She phones Diane a few times a week, usually the moment she gets up. Diane and her daughter swap the usual banter about daily events. It is while they are talking that another call registers on Diane's "call-waiting" service. Diane chooses to ignore it, and continues the conversation with her daughter, whose husband has an affinity for all-terrain vehicles and has been meandering through the Okanagan Valley and the surrounding hills with his cronies. There is snow out there up in the mountains and the fall flowers are abundant.

When Diane says good-bye to her daughter, she checks the recorded message of the ignored call and is informed that her husband Edward Harris is in the intensive care unit of the Royal Victoria Hospital. No other details are given. As Diane places the receiver back, and turns to look at Lily, she has a bewildered look in her eyes. . .

Lily Cormier has offered to drive Diane down to the hospital in Montreal. But first they must both shower and change their clothes.

Lily will also telephone their women friends when she gets home to cancel plans for tea that afternoon at the Ritz-Carlton hotel and the shopping expedition at the underground Place Ville-Marie boutiques. The group had been planning this for quite some time.

Just before noon, Diane Harris enters the hospital and is directed down a series of long corridors to the

Intensive Care Unit, where she is taken by a nurse to the bedside of Edward Harris, her husband of the last twenty-six years. He is sedated and asleep, hardly recognizable, his face pallid and pasty, an oxygen mask covering mouth and nose. The beep of the monitor beside him is soft but eminently audible.

This cannot be her spouse, Diane thinks, a man who left for work a few hours ago. She leans over the gurney next to the IV stand, which holds up the luminous bag of yellowish solvent whose sustenance courses through his system. She immediately thinks of Kathleen in British Columbia who has recently informed them that she is expecting her first child. It occurs to Diane that her stricken husband might not ever see his first grandchild, a possibility that gnaws at her heart. She touches his hand, close to where the IV needle is inserted, securely covered with plasters. His hand is warm. She realizes that she has not reached out to touch his hand in many months. She loves him still, and although their relationship has cooled over the years, she is proud of his success. Now exposed to his helplessness, she feels a swell of resolve.

A doctor comes in and asks Diane to step out into the corridor.

"Mrs. Harris?" he begins. "I'm Doctor Beaulieu. It seems that your husband has suffered a fairly severe coronary occlusion, and we had to use the defibrillator to revive him. But he appears to be stabilized now."

"What are his chances, doctor?"

"Well, the next forty-eight hours should tell us how he will respond. It's difficult to tell right now how much damage to the heart muscle has occurred. How old is your husband?"

159

"He turned fifty-six last June."

"Well, he appears to be strong, and his vital signs are good, so we feel confident that he can pull through this period with close clinical supervision. Later on we can use some procedures, perhaps an angiogram, to get a better picture of what exactly happened and we can go from there. Meanwhile, we'll keep him here for a few days, and if all goes well, we'll transfer him to a regular room."

"Fine, doctor," says Diane.

Doctor Beaulieu is a short compact man with soft eyes. He has been speaking just above a whisper, and exudes a quiet confidence. He has not removed his gaze from Diane's eyes since he began talking to her. She wants to hug him, and tell him that she believes in him, that he has her full support. Her eyes well up.

"So I'll be checking in on him today, Mrs. Harris, and you can rest assured that he will get the best of care."

"Thank you, doctor."

He leaves her and hurries down the hospital corridor. She stands watching him for a few seconds, then turns and goes back into the ICU.

Diane must call her daughter and break the news to her. She will use the cell phone to do this, but she cannot call from inside the hospital. She feels an arm around her waist and turns to see her son, Eddie. She looks up at him as her eyes fill with tears again.

"How is he, Mom?"

"He's gonna be all right. He just needs some rest now."

"But he seemed great this morning. I can't believe it!"

"How did you find out?"

"I phoned Dad at the bank, and they told me. There was a hold-up there this morning. Did you hear?"

"No! I don't believe it!"

"Apparently Dad collapsed in his office during the robbery."

"Oh, my God!"

Diane and Eddie sit outside along the walkway leading to the hospital. A cornucopia of autumnal colour surrounds them. The tall structures of Montreal stand below the hill, the rays of sunlight splashing against some glass-faced buildings in brilliant reflection.

"Hello, Kathleen. Can you hear me?" says Diane into the cell phone. She begins to cry, her body shaking slightly.

Her son takes the phone from her.

"Hi, Kathy. This is Eddie."

Boardwalk

LAST NIGHT STARTED INNOCENTLY ENOUGH. I mean, I was just up around the park, like I often am, looking at the people. It was a hell of a nice evening, warm for this late in August. There I am sitting on this park bench, sort of enjoying myself. From where I'm sitting, I can see the ships down on the river, anchored for the night, all of them lit up like Christmas trees. I wonder why they leave so many lights on at night.

Of course, most of the girls I'm looking over are with guys. Not that I imagine each one as being with me, or anything like that. I just get a charge out of watching a girl and guy walking along, their arms around each other. I even saw a guy and his girlfriend making out one night, not ten feet from where I was sitting. And the funniest thing about it was that the guy knew I was sitting there on a bench behind this clump of bushes. But it didn't seem to bother him a bit. He piled right onto her and even looked at me while in the process.

But getting back to last night, I was also feeling kind of sorry for myself. I mean, I was alone as usual and when you're alone in a park at night time, everybody looks at you as if you're a weirdo or something, as if you're gonna rape the nearest woman or molest some old man. But honestly, I wouldn't hurt a fly. I'm the mildest bastard in the world. I don't think I've ever been

162

in a fight in my life. Any kind of violence just sickens me.

Even arguments upset me, whether I win or lose. Just the other day I got into this wrangle with one of the guys at the office. All because of the goddamn telephone. You see, this guy Len Foley is always on the office phone. Not business calls or anything like that. Personal calls. He spends half the workday on the phone talking to women, and he's married, with two kids. Well, he's a pretty big guy, see, and everybody's scared to say anything to him. So I take it upon myself to tell him.

"You're always on the phone," I said for starters, as soon as he gets off.

"Listen, Corbett," he says, almost leaning on top of me. "You look after your business, and I'll take care of mine."

"But, Len," I tried to reason with him, my voice trembling, "we're supposed to share the work in this office, and you don't do your share. You spend all day on the phone with . . . women. Tell me, Len. How many forms have you processed this afternoon? We were told to work as a team here."

"Lookit, Corbett!" He's almost yelling now. "Do I interfere with your private affairs? Do I tell you what to do up in the park at night? Do I tell you who to hang around with? You do your thing and I'll do mine."

"What do you mean 'at night'? What's that got to do with anything?"

I should have dropped the issue instead of asking for explanations.

"Listen, Corbett," he says. "Everybody knows you hang around with a bunch of queers."

I guess he was just waiting for a chance to say that. I mean, that was really a shocker. Good thing I went to the washroom then, because when it really dawned on me, what he said made me sick to my stomach and I kind of retched. I spent half an hour in the men's room working up the courage to go back and face everybody in the office. It was very quiet for the rest of the afternoon that day.

Things at the office haven't been the same since. I mean, they sort of avoid me. Not that they paid much attention to me in the first place. I think I'll quit that job. Yesterday I tell Mum I'm thinking of leaving.

"Now, Frank, you've been leaving that place for the last ten years," Mum says.

She's right. I've been with the government tax office now for over twelve years. Since I left my college courses. Mum's always right. I mean, since the old man died (my father was an alcoholic), Mum and I have had it pretty good. She works at the Wal-Mart store and we never get in each other's way. But she's always there when I need her. She makes my meals, does my laundry, the whole bit. There's only one thing. Her coffee. She has to have her coffee all the time. She takes down about half a dozen cups every evening, regular. Then she's up half the night because she can't sleep. I know, because we sleep in the same room. We only have a two-and-a-half room apartment.

Still, Mum's great. But she isn't aware. She doesn't give a damn about what's going on. Like last night when I get back from the park, Jean Claude is waiting for me at the apartment. Now, Jean Claude is a little strange, a sort of effeminate type. Like, he talks and walks like a woman, you know, and he swings his hips, and bends his wrist and waves his arms around to express himself. Not that he isn't a nice guy. He is. I mean, he's always lending me money. I don't think I've paid him back most of what he's lent me. But, like I say, Mum just doesn't realize anything about Jean Claude. She thinks he's a charming man. She keeps saying that if she was a young lady, Jean Claude would be her type. But, believe me, he's just not interested in women. Not that he isn't good-looking or anything. Oh, he's a little chubby, mind you. But he's not attracted to girls. He likes guys a whole lot better.

Just to give you an idea of how it is with him, the other night we were sitting on a park bench when these two guys come walking up the path. You see, it's pretty dark there and I'm sitting with Jean Claude doing my best to hold him off. Well, anyway, these two guys are making some racket. They're laughing it up very loud and sort of destroying the atmosphere. And besides, they're staggering around and look sort of drunk.

Well, one of the guys comes right up to our bench and says, very effeminately, "Hiya, fellows," and sort of flaps his wrist at us.

Well, Jesus! Then they both burst into a fit of laughter, which lasted a good while. They're practically rolling on the ground. Of course, I start to get pretty nervous, eh? I mean, these guys are looking for trouble. Believe me, I know their type. They get a great kick out of beating up "queers." My heart starts beating like mad, and I feel like throwing up, and I want to run like hell out of there. But all this doesn't bother Jean Claude. You'd swear he was expecting this kind of behaviour from them. You see, to Jean Claude, everyone is a prospect. I don't give a hell who the guy is, Jean Claude is always looking him over. And though I'm ready to spring up suddenly and bolt out of there, Jean Claude starts up a conversation with these guys.

"I see you fellas are having a good time tonight," says Jean Claude in his high-pitched voice.

As soon as the guys hear his voice they start laughing all over again. I mean, they were really drunk.

"What are you guys doing here anyway?" one of the guys says to us finally.

"We're just sitting here, minding our own business," I answered, and I realized right away that I should have kept my mouth shut. But I was mad as well as scared. I mean, why the hell didn't they leave us alone?

"No, no," says Jean Claude, "don't be angry, Frank. They're nice guys."

"Yeah, shut your fucking trap, you god-damn queer," says the second guy. I mean, he said that as roughly as you can imagine it.

The two guys are standing right over us now. Even if I wanted to run, I couldn't have. Jesus, was I scared! And sweating!

"There's police cars that pass here all the time," I said to them. I didn't sound very convincing.

"The cops should arrest you guys. They should pay us for beating the crap out of you," one of them said.

These guys were young, and one of them had this very short brushcut. They seemed to have sort of British accents. It occurred to me that they might be from one of the ships in port. Both were stocky and I was certain that they would start beating us. There was no way out, so I decided that I would cover up as well as possible if they started punching us.

"You fellas are from one of the ships, eh?" says Jean Claude.

"Yeah, that's right," they answered immediately, together.

Well, Jesus! That did it! The whole scene changed. They sort of hesitated and looked at each other without speaking.

Then one of them said, "Come on, Freddie, let's fuck off."

And they just left us and went off down the path again.

I couldn't believe it! What a relief!

It was like Jean Claude had given them an order to leave.

"That little guy has beautiful blond hair," says Jean Claude, after they had left. He said that just as cool as if nothing had happened. And we had come extremely close to having our heads banged in. I mean, God, was I glad when they took off.

That's one thing about Jean Claude. He's not scared of anyone, even though I hear he's been beaten up more than once. I remember seeing him one day with a big black eye, all puffed up, completely shut. But he was proud of it, and didn't put anything on it, or try to cover it up.

So after that experience with these two sailors, I gained a lot of respect for Jean Claude. I mean, he's fearless. And I was pretty grateful to him for getting us out of that jam, so I let him fool around with me a bit. Just a bit, though, because I just don't go for it too much. I'm a Catholic, you know, and I just don't think it's right or normal. And although Mum doesn't go to church any more, I still go every Sunday. It isn't that I'm religious or anything like that, but I feel that if I give that up, everything else will fall apart. I mean, going to church keeps me from becoming like Jean Claude, I'm positive.

And like I was saying, last night Jean Claude was waiting for me, talking to Mum, and he was wearing this outfit that looks like the sailor suits that kids wear. Well, he wanted to go up to the boardwalk just for a stroll. Now, this boardwalk is something to see if you haven't been there. There's hundreds of people walking on it when the weather is nice. Everybody's there: tourists, pickpockets, prostitutes, everybody. Don't get me wrong. It's a lovely boardwalk, overlooking the river below, a cool breeze blowing in your face, lots of people well dressed, even a brass band sometimes earlier in the evening.

But I'm not too keen on being seen with Jean Claude, with him dressed in that outfit. But on the other hand, I've got to get him away from Mum. I just can't stomach that, him pulling the wool over her eyes like he does. It's just too much. So I start out for the boardwalk with him. But I just can't get comfortable walking beside him. I'm wearing a gray tweed suit coat with a white shirt and tie, and he's got this red-white-and-blue sailor suit on. This is not the first time I've felt this way about us walking together.

And god-dammit, who do you think I run into on the sidewalk on our way up to the boardwalk, eh? That's right, Len Foley! You know, the guy at the office. He's walking along with this other guy and when he catches sight of me and Jean Claude, he gives me a "haven't I got you pegged" look which makes me feel like less than two cents. I could see him coming from a distance and I hoped he wouldn't catch sight of us. But no such luck. Not only that, but just as he passes me, he lets out this low horse laugh of his. It wouldn't have been so bad if Jean Claude hadn't been walking so close to me, but of course that's the way he always walks with me, rubbing his hip against me all the time. The guy has got incredible energy.

By the time we get to the boardwalk, it's pretty late, about midnight, but there's still a lot of people around. I like it up there, it's relaxing, you're sort of lost in the crowd, and it's fairly dimly lit. As I said, it was a beautiful night, with the big yellow moon and all. I mean, I like it up there, once I'm there.

A half-hour after walking up and down the boardwalk, I'm getting pretty thirsty. So I convince Jean Claude to come into the boardwalk lounge for a beer. It's part of the big hotel there. Jean Claude doesn't like the idea too much. I mean, I hardly ever go into places like that. Mostly I hang around the park, or watch television at night. God, can I watch TV! I can watch TV for ten hours straight without moving. I lose myself in front of the TV set.

So we go into the boardwalk lounge and the place is really jumping. There's a combo playing for about a hundred people dancing in a space about five feet square, and it's pretty dark in the place. This big bouncer-type guy takes us into a corner and seats us at a table with these two girls.

No sooner are we seated when Jean Claude takes out these pornographic pictures from his pocket and wants to show them to me. Of course, that wasn't the place to look at these things. First of all, it was too dark in there. Not that I don't like looking at them, to be honest. I've got some at home. But Jean Claude has these pictures showing kids in pornographic poses. I think he could be arrested for that. I think he scans them from the Internet. I swear that's the way he makes his living, selling them to people. But if he ever got caught, he could go to jail for years.

One of the girls at the table with us is feeling pretty high and she's snapping her fingers to the music. She seems to know or remember Jean Claude from somewhere. So before long, she and Jean Claude are looking at his pictures and giggling and they've hit it off pretty well. I don't know what to think about them because I'm sure he's not interested in her.

The other girl refuses to look at the pictures. After I was served a beer, I looked at the other girl out of the corner of my eye. She's not bad at all. She's got no chest to speak of, but her face is pretty good-looking. She's got one of those sleeveless dresses on and her arms are brown and well formed. Not that she's a young chick or anything like that. She's not. I'd say she's about twenty-seven or twenty-eight or so. I was trying to decide whether to buy her a drink or not. But I think the thing to do is to ask a girl to dance first and then offer her a drink. But you're not going to see me up on the dance floor trying to do those god-damn dances. I haven't danced with anybody for twenty years, not since I danced with Aunt Martha at Mum's wedding anniversary party.

I took my beer down real fast and ordered another one. I noticed that the girl was taking quick peeks at me. That gave me courage.

"Can I buy you a drink?" I ask her.

"Oh. Oh, all right." she says.

For some reason Jean Claude gets up and leaves the table then, after giving me one of those quick discouraged looks. I mean, he can really get jealous. But the trouble with Jean Claude is that he takes a lot for granted. I been hanging around with him for about six months now and he calls me up at least three times a day, even calls to the office which I don't like the idea of. A few weeks ago we're over at his place looking at pictures and watching television, and just taking it easy, which I like to do. All of a sudden, he puts his hand on my leg and says, "Frank, why don't you move your things in here with me?"

I told him I couldn't, that I wanted to stay with Mum and help her pay the rent and all. Believe it or not, Jean Claude started to sulk. I mean, he refused to talk to me any more that night. He wouldn't even say "goodnight" when I left. Then the next day he calls me at the office as if nothing had happened. That's what I mean. He can get pretty possessive at times. Not that I'm sorry I met him. He's really a very generous guy.

But getting back to this boardwalk lounge place, as I say, Jean Claude gets up and leaves me with these two girls. Then, almost right away, a guy comes over and asks the girl, the one who was talking to Jean Claude, to dance. So I'm left with the girl I was telling you about. I don't think I've ever sat with a girl in a bar before, so this is a new experience for me.

Of course, I wanted to get a conversation going but I couldn't think of how to start. So we just sat there for a while. Finally I said, "The music is pretty loud, eh?"

"Yes," she agrees.

"What's your name?" I was really opening up.

"Teresa Kelso," she says, pronouncing it very carefully, leaning toward me.

That reminded me of my old man. His name was Terrence, but he was never in any condition to pronounce anything correctly. I mean, he was drunk all the time. He used to come home at about eleven every night.

He never showed up for supper, and later when he did show up, he'd start an argument with Mum, and he used to beat her quite often. Of course, I was always in bed by this time but I couldn't ever sleep. I used to lie awake waiting for him to stagger in, and hope the argument wouldn't start. Hope? God, I was terrified that they would start arguing! It was hardly ever Mum's fault, although she could use pretty nasty language. They yelled a lot at each other. The neighbours would phone up at the height of an argument and my old man would curse at them over the phone. We lived in one of those second-floor tenements then, and even in winter you could hear what was going on in the next flat.

One night the old man staggered in, after storming up the stairway. He went to the kitchen right away and turned on the tap. Then he went into the bathroom and opened the medicine cabinet and knocked down several bottles that broke on the bathroom tiles and the sink. Mum jumped up out of bed and rushed into the bathroom.

"What in Jesus do you think you're doing?" she just about screamed.

She never had a chance to say more. I could hear several loud slaps as the old man really gave it to her. I jumped out of bed then and ran into the hallway outside the bathroom and tried to pull him away from her. I was fourteen years old then, and not very strong. Yet I was still able to upset him so that he fell onto the floor in the kitchen. When he turned around to look at me, I could see that there was blood all over his face. He must have gotten into a fight at the tavern before coming home. Anyway, he starts laughing hysterically, and then breaks into sobbing. I think it was just about two weeks after that that he died. Funny thing, for those last two weeks there was no fighting in the house. My father died at the mill where he worked. They found him behind a pile of crates in the warehouse, Mum tells me.

But this Theresa Kelso is not a bad-looking girl at all. I mean, she's got a nice smile.

"This is the first time I come into this place," I said. "I've seen it from the outside a hundred times. Are you a regular here?"

"Oh, no. I've come in just a few times with my friend Cecile. She likes to dance."

She half-turned to look toward the dance floor. We could both see her friend still whooping it up with the same fellow who had asked her to dance.

Then Theresa looked back at me and smiled. She's got nice teeth. I don't know if they're real or not, but they're clean, at least. If there's anything I can't stand, it's dirty teeth on anyone. That's another thing about Mum. She always made me brush my teeth. Sometimes you get these real good-looking people—I mean, with good features and all—but when they smile, the whole face changes because they don't take care of their teeth. I mean, that's really stupid, as far as I'm concerned.

Anyway, at first Theresa wasn't helping out much in our conversation. I was asking all the questions. Of course, I suppose she was afraid that I would ask her to dance, which I had no intention of doing because I know I don't look very good dancing. For that matter, I don't look very good just walking, either. One of my legs never came back to normal after my bicycle accident so I have to sort of drag it along after me. That's one thing I like about Jean Claude. He couldn't care less about how I look.

The accident happened about six months before the old man died. I was just turning onto St. John Street when this city bus hit me. I mean, my tires were worn down and the pavement was wet and slippery, so my brakes didn't work too well. Actually, the bus didn't hit me. I hit the bus on the side, and the back wheel of the bus ran over my leg, and hit my head too, Mum tells me. I was in a coma for a week and my leg was broken in about ten places. The accident often came up in the arguments between my old man and Mum. I mean, it was Mum's idea that I get the bike. The old man always said it was too dangerous to ride a bike around where we lived then. I guess he was right.

Neither Jean Claude nor the other girl came back to our table, so I was stuck with Teresa. At least, that's how I felt at the time. I started feeling very self-conscious about myself, and I wanted to leave and just walk back home alone. But I would have preferred if she left the table first, so that she wouldn't see me limp away, because although I can walk fairly fast and even run, I can't hide my limp. It's just impossible. It's part of me now, and I just have to accept it.

"Where do you work?" I asked Theresa.

"I work for Fortin et Giroux. They're insurance brokers," she answered quickly.

"What kind of work do you do?"

"Oh, I do lots of things. Computer stuff, filing, correspondence. Just about everything."

"How long have you been there?" I asked, which was a stupid question, really.

"Oh, quite a while now," she said, and then she smiled again.

Then she stood up, excused herself, and headed for the ladies' room, I guess, because she left her sweater hanging on the back of the chair. I watched her move away, working her way around the tables and people toward the washroom area. She was quite slim, and very nicely tanned, and I began to imagine her in the nude, her clean white breasts and her little white ass, compared to her brown legs and arms. Since I look at some of these skin pictures, I never fail to imagine almost any girl naked. Fat ones and skinny ones, old and young, tall and short. You name it, I can picture it.

By the time she gets back from the washroom, I'm on my third beer, and I'm starting to feel pretty good. She's not a very fast drinker. She's hardly touched the drink I bought her. Then I realize that I have to go for a leak myself. I mean, I'm going to have to get up now, I'm busting. So, what the hell, I do get up, and walk over toward the men's room, doing my best to limp as little as possible. She can't fail to notice it. When she sees it, she'll take off. By this time, I'm not so sure if I want her to leave. I'm feeling fairly high even if I am sorry for myself, and I'm sorta enjoying her company.

There's a whole bunch of guys waiting in front of the urinals, so I have to line up and wait my turn. And I'm asking myself if she'll be still at the table when I get back. Because, for some bloody reason, this is the big test. I mean, if she doesn't leave, maybe she doesn't mind being with me.

And good Christ! When I work my way back to the table, I can see she's still there. She's sitting and, although she's facing me, she's looking in another direction. I mean, she's doing that on purpose, because she doesn't want to embarrass me. Most people I know don't look at me when I approach them. They avoid my eyes. But people do stare at me from the side or from behind. I just know it. I can feel it. People like to look at my limp without my noticing them.

As I sit myself down again, she gives me that little smile, and it makes me feel sort of funny all over.

"Well, it's getting late, and I think I'll have to go now," she says.

"Where do you live?" I ask.

"On Olivier, just near Côte d'Abraham."

"Well, look. I'm taking a cab home. Maybe I can drop you off?"

She hesitates for a moment.

"All right," she says, at last.

I mean, I'm really taking a girl home. This has never happened to me. I don't believe it!

So we step out onto the boardwalk from the noisy lounge and start walking toward the taxi stand which is at the entrance of the boardwalk. She's wearing high-heeled shoes and is just a little shorter than I am. As we walk down the boardwalk, we're not saying anything, but her footsteps are tapping pretty evenly on the boards while mine are sort of irregular as usual. I mean, that says a lot.

"Do you want to sit down for a while?" I ask her.

"Oh, all right. Just for a minute," she says.

So we sit on the bench facing the river and for the first time I can smell her. What I mean is, I can get a whiff of her perfume and it's really nice, not that cheap stuff that women spray on sometimes which just about turns my stomach. And we're sitting pretty close together, too. I mean, her shoulder and mine are actually touching. And, like I said, it's really nice up there, real romantic and everything. And then she asks me where I work and all, and I told her about my job and about

Mum and the old man and about my accident and everything. And God, you know, we really got to talking. We must have been there for over an hour. Theresa is a hell of a nice girl. I mean, we're going to the movies tomorrow night. Jeez, I haven't been to a movie house in years.

Meg

I'M NOT SURE OF THE DATE I first saw her last spring, but it was in the elevator of the Royal Bank building in downtown Montreal. I was coming back home from a job interview at some advertising agency. They were looking for a person with a "creative mind" and "fresh ideas." Hey, I said to myself, who's got a more contemporary view of the revolving cosmos than Hardy Knox? So I'd headed there on a sort of a lark.

I'd just graduated from the Education Faculty at McGill University and was looking for a full-time position as a school teacher. But at that particular time there seemed to be few openings in the Montreal area for a math teacher at an English-language school.

So why not look for some other job while waiting?

I don't have to tell you how claustrophobic you can get in a gorged elevator. I suppose if all these people who are with you in this gravitating projectile were members of your own family, you could make the most of it.

"Hey, Uncle Howard. Isn't it great to be so close to your relatives?"

But the truth is that, in travel by Otis, you are compressed into a diversity of humanoids, all of whom you have never met, nor are likely to ever meet again.

The silence can be overpowering.

On the afternoon I first saw Meg, my view of her

could be described as extreme close-up. I was standing sort of perpendicular to her, facing her profile, if you can picture that. I could not really move without destroying the still-life ambiance, which the elevator passengers had configured for this trip down from the 21st floor to the lobby. To move to a less vulnerable position would have created a rush of acoustic signal power easily surpassing the pain level.

So Meg and I maintained our geographic locations, my loins occasionally brushing her clothing as we hurtled downward.

Since my mouth was approximately six inches from her ear, I stopped breathing as I normally do, yet allowed limited amounts of carbon to escape from my nose, and I was thankful I hadn't just eaten strong salami or garlic, which I happen to like.

Needless to say, she looked rather beautiful—or, beautiful rather than anything else. Everything about her, from her dark hair and eyes to her full blossoming lips, chastened me somewhat. Why had fate chosen me to be compacted in an elevator beside such a sensuous-looking girl? And that fragrance she emitted was so correct, so perfect.

But she was looking up at the ceiling of this descending capsule and never actually moved her eyeballs to meet mine.

When the passengers evacuated into the huge lobby, I watched her walk away, out of my life forever, deprived of the incalculable pleasure of knowing me.

The next time I saw her was at least six months later, at Dooley's, a west-island pub and restaurant not far from my home. I was there with about six other guys, still sweating from a touch football game we'd played, drinking down a few beers, being sort of loud and raucous, trying hard to replace the calories we'd lost on the field.

Since the place was so noisy and busy, I'm surprised I even noticed her. She was sitting about four tables away with two other girls.

I said to "Blame" Kelly, "See that dark girl over there with the white sweater?"

We call him "Blame" because he's always dropping the football in the end zone.

"Yeah," says Blame.

"Where?" I asked.

"Where what?" he asked.

"Where have I seen her before?"

And then it hit me. I felt a surge in my chest, which always happens when a profound and spiritual inspiration is aroused in me.

"Wait, Hardy. I mean, has she seen you before?"

"We're not sure," I said, "I saw her in an elevator downtown."

The other guys soon gained access to our little exchange and since everybody was suitably beered up, and despite my pleas, Walter Fortin, six-feet-four, two hundred and sixty pounds, self-appoints himself to walk over to the table where the girls are, to inform the "dark-haired" one that a guy back at his table has seen her before.

As I was still sober enough to be petrified, I hung my head.

All the guys are looking over at the table as Walter is animatedly gesticulating, and then pointing back to me. The three girls, all of whom appear to know Walter, are giggling and obviously enjoying the moment. We can't make out what's being said because of the din.

Soon Walter is back.

"Vell, Valter?" says Blame, "Vat did she say?"

"The girls say that they've never seen your ugly face before, Hardy!" announces Walter.

Everybody roars with laughter.

Walter goes on, "Actually, Hardy, the dark one says she saw you downtown some time ago. Her name is Meg Watson, in case you're interested."

I couldn't believe it! How could she even remember?

Of course, we kept joking and drinking beer for a while after that, but I couldn't get my mind straightened out. I looked over at their table every few minutes but never quite met her eyes even if her chair was facing mine and the visual path was unimpaired.

I had to relieve myself then, and since the men's room was beyond their table, there was no way I could avoid getting closer to her.

When I got up, I suppose she thought I was heading over to speak to her, so she smiled up at me.

"Sorry you didn't get that job," she said.

"The job? What job?" I barked.

"Didn't you apply for a job at Ross and Tremblay's in the spring? You know, the advertising people?"

"Oh, yeah. Of course." I snapped my fingers, a really cool habit I have.

"I used to work there. I saw you come in, I remember."

"I didn't luck out on that one," I said.

"On the contrary. I think you did, by not getting caught up with them."

The other girls laughed at this remark.

Hearing them laugh really opened up the floodgates.

"My name is Hardy Knox," I said, looking at the other girls. "I saw Meg a little while ago, so I, eh, er . . ." I began to babble and sputter, literally, to which the girls responded with more mirthful tittering.

Meg then told me the names of the other girls.

Then I said, "Could you give me a phone number where I can reach you?"

I couldn't believe I'd said it. The beer had loosened my tongue and thrown my inhibitions to the winds.

"Yes, of course," Meg said.

She borrowed a pen and a slip of torn-off envelope from one of her pals and gave me a phone number.

When I got back to the table, exalted beyond description, flushed with elation, Blame asked me why I had leaked all over my jeans.

I spent the next few days summoning up the courage to call her, thinking that, with her looks, there must be a waiting list of guys who wanted to take her out. I figured I'd ask her to go to a movie, but I wanted to make sure I could get my dad's car for the occasion.

My dad sells insurance for a living. He works hard, and never misses an opportunity to make a contact. He's out a lot in the evenings, and it's hard to predict if the car will be available. My mom also uses the car because of her work at St. Leo's Parish church here in Pointe Claire, where she's on just about every committee.

So I get around by bus a lot of the time, or take the train when I go into Montreal. Or one of the guys picks me up in his car.

The telephone number Meg had given me was not her home number, but the number at the book store where she worked. I called her the next Friday evening when the store was still open. She said she was very busy and couldn't talk, but agreed to accompany me to a movie the following Monday evening. She gave me her home address and I agreed to pick her up at around 7:00 p.m.

Meg Watson's house was on Lakeshore Drive in Beaconsfield. It so happened that I couldn't persuade my dad to re-schedule an appointment he had with a client.

"Hardy, we're talking about a $3,000 commission here!" my dad said, with finality.

But I didn't have the courage to phone Meg and tell her that we were going to the movies on the bus.

When I found her house facing the river, I was astounded by the size of the place, surrounded by autumn-coloured trees and with several cars parked neatly in a rather exaggerated paved area.

A tall young guy answered the door.

"Hi, I'm Bernard. Come on in. Meg will be . . . Meg?" he called back.

Bernard walked away before I could tell him what my name was and just as I was about to offer my hand. I slipped inside and closed the door.

I was in a sort of anteroom that was about the size of the living room at my home. From what I could see of this house, I was obviously out of my class. Everything about this mansion—the chandeliered lighting, the ornately framed pictures on the walls, the rich lustre of the deep inside of the house—emanated wealth.

There was a small velvet settee in the anteroom, so I cautiously sat on it, just as Bernard came back.

"She'll be down in a few minutes," he said curtly.

"All right, thank you," I tried to tell him but he was gone again.

I wasn't too impressed with Bernard. He had that haughty look about him. He was at least six-feet-three and literally looked down at me, even if he didn't have as athletic a build as I have.

Then Meg walked into the anteroom. She looked like one of the models from the pages of *Seventeen* magazine which my sisters used to buy.

Just for an instant I wondered what I was doing there, but the smile she gave me soon caused my feeling of inadequacy to fade somewhat.

"You look great," I uttered, in my bottomless appreciation.

"So do you," she said.

I decided to come right out with it.

"I couldn't get my dad's car tonight, so I thought we'd just take the . . ."

"That's okay. We can use mine. I'll go get the keys."

She was gone again, and another of the world's great dark clouds evaporated.

She allowed me to drive her late model 4-wheel drive Suburu to the Cineplex. I was sorry then that I'd chosen a movie for our first evening out. It meant that I couldn't gaze at her, fawning the whole evening. I'd have done better by bringing her to a bar, where I could've faced her, secretly glorifying to myself and to everyone else around that I was in the company of this lovely person.

Once seated beside her at the movie, however, it seemed paramount that I demonstrate to her what a gentleman I was. No gaucherie, I said to myself. Don't start slobbering all over her. Keep your hands to yourself. Wait till she makes a move indicating that she's comfortably pleased to be in my company. I felt that I'd not always played my cards right in a few past dates with girls, even if, at twenty-four years of age, I have developed a suitable quantity of self-esteem.

When I looked at Meg, and caught the scent of her, there was an essence of the ethereal in my feeling. This was the first time I'd met a girl that I genuinely did not want to lose.

The movie itself was an attack on common sense. It concerned a veteran police officer struggling with the forces of evil. After a series of investigative events during one typical urban day, he manages to get drunk in a downtown bar. He is in uniform all this time. He meets an attractive woman at this bar, then takes her to his one-half room apartment where he is temporarily living while he is in the process of divorce proceedings.

I did hold Meg's hand, on and off, during the movie. Her response was warm, if a little tentative.

On our way back home, we stopped off at a fast food restaurant and had coffee.

"Well, what did you think of the movie?" I asked.

"Typically Hollywood, very good action, high quality from a technical point of view. But I found the characters a little hard to swallow. They don't wash before they make love."

We both laughed at her remark.

"My exact feeling," I said. "I was thinking the same thing."

Redundancy is one of my strong cards.

"You know," she went on, "I can understand why some Hollywood stars refuse to watch their own movies."

We talked about movies in general and what, if any, effect they had on society. It wasn't the kind of conversation I'd expected. But then, she did work at a book store.

"I love reading books," she said. "I love reading book titles. I can go into any book store and spend hours just reading the titles of books and the blurbs on the back cover."

Her eyes floated upwards in a swooning look.

She asked about my touch-football mates who'd been at the bar. She wanted to know who they were, and if they were still in school or working. She said she knew Walter Fortin's younger sister. They'd gone to John Rennie High School together.

I inquired about her dad's business.

"My dad wants me to get involved in the construction business. But I find it hard to get excited about building warehouses, or the cost analysis of cement or steel, and all those things. I almost have my BA, just a few more courses to go. But my major is Can. Lit. and my dad always laughed at that. He wanted me to be an engineer. But I always detested math and physics. I'm too much of a romantic for that stuff."

"Hey, wait a minute!" I faked protestation. "I love math! I'd like to teach math and maybe even trig in high school. Are you saying that I'm not very romantic?"

She laughed again and reached across the small table and squeezed my forearm with both her hands.

"No, Hardy! I'm sorry! I didn't mean that!"

I loved it when she said my name.

"Well, watch that, Meg! You're not being politically correct. I'm very sensitive about this abasement of those who love the sciences and the Newtonian theories."

She laughed then, again, a deep lovable laugh starting from deep down within her.

"No! No!" she kept saying, "You don't understand, Hardy!"

"This constant pummelling from the artistic and intellectual elite has got to stop. Who built the bridges in this country? Mordecai Richler? Ezra Pound? Who is testing the frontiers of space? Woody Allen?"

"Stop, Hardy! Those people over there are staring at me!"

She took a kleenex from her handbag and wiped her eyes, still laughing.

I wanted her to laugh some more, to enjoy me. I felt as if I was on a roll, that I couldn't miss.

I did not see Meg for at least two weeks after that. On two attempts to take her out to dinner, I fell short. She declined both times, saying she had previous commitments with her family.

In the meantime, in early October, I landed a job teaching in an elementary school in Pierrefonds, another suburb just north of Pointe Claire. While not on permanent staff, I began substituting for a female teacher who'd been involved in an automobile accident, and whose prospects for a return to the classroom did not seem propitious.

Up to that point, I'd worked selling shoes at a Bay outlet, as well as cashiering at a self-service gas station. This wasn't work that I was particularly proud of, but beggars can't be choosers, my dad always said.

Few teachers can forget their first legitimate classroom job, I suppose, and I was no exception. I'd faced different grade levels during my student-teaching phase. I'd always intended to teach high school, but I soon discovered that I really enjoyed the elementary school students. The grade five kids I have are bright, and precocious, and seem to revel in the humour which I dispense, perhaps too generously.

I love to get up in the morning and go to my teaching job.

Most of the teachers at Good Shepherd, where I work, are in their forties and fifties, some close to retirement, so the landscape looks promising.

"There's a sweet-voiced female who's been trying to reach you since four o'clock. She's called three times, I think. Meg, is it?" My mom announced as I walked in the door.

"Oh!" I almost shouted.

I immediately went to my room, closed the door, and threw myself on my bed.

"Yes! Yes! Yes!" I screamed into my pillow.

Of course, I'd thought up the worst scenarios regarding Meg. She'd decided I didn't smell too good. I had sweaty palms, and I didn't even know how to dress properly. There was no way she was gonna hang around with a god-damn teacher who didn't even have his own car. How could she be even seen with a guy who fitted shoes on little old ladies at the Bay?

But, again, I was wrong, wrong, wrong!

Before I could return her call, she called me again, inviting me to dine at her house, to meet her mom and dad, even.

I spent the next few days in a state of slight emotional upheaval. My younger sisters got word of my new romantic interest and made a collage for me with their old Valentine cards.

"Do I look okay, Mom?" I said, on the fateful evening.

I had my best and only suit on, something charcoal grey I'd bought for my university graduation ceremony. I was also wearing a pink shirt, and one of my dad's best ties.

"You look spiffy, dear," she said, patting me on the butt.

My dad was sitting in his favourite chair, balancing his glass of Chivas Regal.

"That one of my ties?" he asked.

"Your son has been invited out to dinner," Mother informed him.

"Oh? Where at, Hardy?"

"I'm about to meet the Watson clan at an informal dinner."

"Look out, son. When they invite you to meet mother, it's serious business."

My dad got up and poured more Scotch into his glass from the decanter.

My dad loves Scotch. Probably too much, though not as much as my Uncle Howard, who is my dad's twin brother. They are, of course, very close. They even like to dress the same, would you believe it? My Uncle Howard will tell my dad, for example, that he is going out to A. Gold & Sons to buy a suit.

"Hughie, I'm getting a suit made with this great new material. There's a blue pin stripe in it. It's kind of grey," Uncle Howard will say.

And sure enough, my dad will head up to the same tailor a few days later and order the exact same get-up.

These men are in their middle fifties!

My dad and Uncle Howard are pretty well known on the West Island. They both were super athletes, especially in hockey and football, in their younger days.

Uncle Howard is a pretty successful entrepreneur in Quebec. He shares ownership in bars and restaurants, as well as a few shopping malls.

I've always considered him to be over-energized, a guy who can glad-hand with the best, but who can push PR to ridiculous proportions. It is said that he will rebuke people for not finishing up their meals at some of his restaurants.

"Something wrong with the food?" he'll say.

My dad, Hugh Francis Knox, is more laid-back than his brother Howard, but still very outgoing, still with a wee wild streak in him.

They both still play hockey once a week with the old-timers during the winter season.

My mom has always expressed a certain wariness about Uncle Howard, feeling that he is always slightly drunk, and unpredictable. She says that Uncle Howard is headed for a premature heart attack, and suspects that my dad will have one just to emulate Uncle Howard. But her warnings to my dad have gone on for years and Uncle Howard still remains a strong influence on my dad.

My dinner date at Meg's house did not exactly turn out the way I expected.

First of all, when I drove up to the house, I couldn't get into their parking lot—there were too many cars there—Jaguars, Cadillacs, and other expensive models.

This turned out to be a cocktail and buffet, held mostly in the back patio and swimming pool area. There seemed to be a lot of guests at this get-together, so I sort of felt a little out of place walking in.

But Meg came out of the front door with a look of relief on her face.

"Oh, Hardy! I thought you'd never get here!" she said, and she threw her arms around my neck.

"Why? Am I late?" I protested. "I think I'm right on time."

"Why are you all dressed up? You must be so warm!"

She made me take off my suit coat and tie. It was a pretty balmy early October evening.

"I'm sorry, Hardy. I should have told you to wear something casual."

Come to think of it, she had told me it was to be an informal evening.

"Sorry, Meg. I'm such a klutz!"

"No, Hardy. It's all my fault."

She led me around the house and through a flower-adorned trellis into their back yard. A whole bunch of guests were already lolling in the chairs of a spacious patio area that overlooked the St. Lawrence River. There was a medium-sized swimming pool with a diving board and slide. Hollywood stars would have envied this setting.

Meg then took my hand and pulled me toward a group of people standing with glasses in their hands.

"Come meet my father," she said.

Arthur Watson and his wife, Eleanor, were a rather impressive looking couple. He appeared to be somewhat shorter than she, and was built like a construction man, with thick hairy forearms and a huge powerful hand, which I shook. Eleanor, who was dressed in a pale yellow outfit, only gave me a token salutation and did not extend her hand to me. But she did smile at the others as she greeted me. She didn't appear to be moved enough by my presence to really look at me.

"Just make yourself at home," she said.

This was apparently a catered event; I noticed people in white jackets laying platters of food on a large table just inside the house.

Of course, it turned out to be a great evening. Meg got hold of a pair of her brother's bathing trunks for me, and we went into the heated pool together with a few of the children who were there. I did a few flips off the diving board and had the cocktail crowd applauding and asking for an encore. Meg and I then splashed around in the pool with some of the children, mostly cousins of hers.

I really got a good look at Meg as she came out of the pool, water dripping from her Speedo-type swimsuit, but I didn't want to be caught staring after her with all the people sitting around the pool. So I treated Meg's presence with a mien of nonchalance, even if I was practically bursting inside.

I wanted to scream out: "Meg, you're the most beautiful thing I've ever seen. Can I please spend the rest of my life with you?"

They allowed me to use one of their sumptuous bathrooms to get dressed again, and a few minutes later I was drinking cold beer and eating hors d'oeuvres. Then we lined up, army style, filed into the house, and loaded up plates from the buffet table.

I didn't get a chance to talk to Meg's parents, really. They were too busy looking after guests. Meg was also quite attentive to some of the people. I kidded around with her young cousins a lot, standing on the grass at pool's edge.

"Do you do weights?" one little guy asked me.

"No, not really. Why?"

"Cause you really have lots of muscles."

"Well, I got those playing sports like hockey and football and baseball."

"How come girls don't have big muscles?" said his little female partner.

"Oh, I don't know. Look at Meg here. She's got lots of muscles."

Meg laughed at this, and wrapped her hands around my throat as if to throttle me. The children enjoyed this ploy and giggled. Then Meg brought her arms down and hugged me, pressing herself against my hip.

"I think Meg loves you," said the little girl.

At this point the cocktail-and-buffet crowd began to lose a little decorum. One lady, teetering too close to the pool, fell in, and as she reached up to some guy to be helped out, she pulled him in. After a while there were four or five of them in the pool. Loud laughter punctuated these shenanigans and from that time on things loosened up a lot and I felt more relaxed about these people.

It started to get cool after a while and most of the guests moved to inside the house. The children just faded away, somehow. Meg and I sat on the padded deck chairs around the pool, sipping drinks and talking.

"So you went to St. Thomas High," Meg said.

"Yep. I'm Catholic, you know. Do you belong to any church or denomination?"

"My mother is Presbyterian. I go to her church sometimes. My father hasn't seen the inside of a church since he went to some wedding last spring. So he just doesn't go to worship, although he was baptized in the Anglican Church."

The water in the pool made that lapping sound, and a chilly breeze rustled the leaves as the sky darkened.

Meg went into the house to get a sweater and when she returned we snuggled together on one of the canopied swing seats. She wrapped her fingers into mine and leaned her head on my shoulder.

"How come you're so beautiful?" I said.

"Didn't you get a good look at my mom?" she countered.

"Yeah, she's gorgeous. I'm just glad you don't have arms like your father's."

"Well, you have arms like my father. You men are all alike, flaunting yourselves whenever you get the chance. My father hates to wear anything that'll hide his arms. He likes to roll up his sleeves all the time and remind people that he's a working man."

"Your dad reminds me of my Uncle Howard. He looks like he's ready for a scrap anytime."

"No. My dad is very calm. He doesn't get excited very easily."

We rocked together gently in the light breeze. I didn't want to be awakened from this dream.

"This is the fourth time we've been together," I reminded her.

"When I saw you come into the office in the spring, I felt a little sorry for you. You looked a little nervous," she said.

"Funny, how did I miss you? Where were you?"

"I was at the photocopy machine, running stuff off. It makes such a racket I thought you'd look over my way, but you didn't."

"You know where I saw you first, eh?"

"No. Where?"

"In the elevator."

"Yes, yes, I remember getting into the elevator right after you. It was so packed. Elevators are so weird."

"Tell me about it."

People were beginning to leave. I did not want to leave.

"Can I sleep here tonight?" I asked, facetiously.

"No. Definitely not."

"I'll stay outside here on one of these padded chairs."

"My dad will dump you into the pool."

"See? I told you. He can be a violent man."

"You're crazy, Hardy! Absolutely bonkers!"

"Tell me, Meg. What is that perfume you're wearing?"

"Do you like it?"

"Yes, it's very stimulating, very motivating."

"All right, since you like it so much, I'll bet you can figure out what it's called."

She snickered during this exchange, trying to talk at the same time.

" Where is it from?" I asked.

"It's from Morocco."

"Is it named after a flower?"

"No. It's named after an animal."

"Is it called 'fragrance of camel'?"

She was laughing a little out of control by now, and threw her arms around me.

"Oh, Hardy! You make me so happy!"

We both stopped laughing then and she kissed me on the cheek first, and then on my mouth. She had full, soft lips and we held that first kiss for quite a while.

"Good night, Meg!" a voice called from across the pool.

I awakened from my stupor, Meg took my hand, and we went over to say good-night to some of the guests.

Later, after we walked to my dad's car, which was parked down the street, I stood with Meg, leaning against the car, holding her around the waist, unwilling to let go of her.

As I was driving off, Meg called to me.

"Hardy!"

"What?"

"Hardy, I forgot to ask you about your teaching job!" she was almost shouting from the sidewalk.

"I'll give you a report card." I yelled back.

She laughed, and I drove off.

Of course, I didn't sleep very well that night. Meg's perfume was still on me and there was no way I was gonna take a shower.

Living close to Montreal, as we do in the West Island, is a mixed blessing. As you grow up and go through the elementary and high school experience, you sense that there is a factor about life in Quebec that must be eventually faced. That factor in Quebec is the French language. So, even if you are raised as an anglophone and communicate in English with your family and friends, the French language looms on the horizon and then imposes itself on your everyday quest for economic survival. The laws and regulations of the province at the political and economic level do not leave much room for those who will not face this factor.

Since the vast majority of the people of Quebec are French-speaking, the expectancy is that you will join them by learning their language. The official language of Quebec is French.

This situation is difficult for a person who immerses herself in North American English-speaking culture, which is so all-pervasive. Some see the French regulations as an obstacle. It is easier for some to move away from Quebec to places where no French requirement is needed.

So when Meg announced to me a few days ago that she'd been offered a promotion by her company, a nation-wide bookselling firm, I was happy to hear it. But when she added that the new job was in Edmonton, Alberta, I felt that surge in my chest again.

These events can make a cynic out of a guy.

But why wouldn't the company want to hang onto her? She has the whole package: brains, looks, an obvious love of books.

"I've got to try this out, Hardy!" she explained.

I suppose I'm fortunate in some ways. My parents sent me and my sisters to French elementary school, so that we'd have a good basic education in French. We then switched to an English high school. So my family is quite comfortable with French even if I don't read Molière on a regular basis.

Meg and I will be writing to each other and talking on the phone. She'll be home for Christmas to spend a week or so.

The guys are riding me a lot about the fact that Meg has left town. Blame Kelly says he has Doctor Kevorkian's phone number if I want it.

On the good side of my life, the school principal where I teach told me that my job is secure till next June, and that, since some teachers are retiring, he thinks he can place me on permanent staff. Besides, I'm the only male teacher on the staff of Good Shepherd Elementary School.

Marquis Book Printing Inc.

Québec, Canada
2008